MATTHEW RIEF

PREDATOR IN THE KEYS
A Logan Dodge Adventure

Florida Keys Adventure Series
Volume 7

D1529045

Logan Dodge Adventures

Gold in the Keys
(Florida Keys Adventure Series Book 1)

Hunted in the Keys
(Florida Keys Adventure Series Book 2)

Revenge in the Keys
(Florida Keys Adventure Series Book 3)

Betrayed in the Keys
(Florida Keys Adventure Series Book 4)

Redemption in the Keys
(Florida Keys Adventure Series Book 5)

Corruption in the Keys
(Florida Keys Adventure Series Book 6)

Predator in the Keys
(Florida Keys Adventure Series Book 7)

If you're interested in receiving my newsletter
for updates on my upcoming books, you can sign up
on my website:

matthewrief.com

PROLOGUE

Gulf of Mexico
1999

The low-profile go-fast boat raced across the water, leaving a long trail of bubbles in its moonlit wake. It appeared in a noisy blur, then vanished into the dark horizon. There one moment and gone the next. Like the passing of a low-flying fighter jet.

Below deck, a middle-aged man with dark skin and midnight-black hair stood hunched over the helm. A wiry young man sat beside him, staring at a small panel of screens. The control space was just big enough for two. The sleek, narrow-hulled craft had been custom designed with two major purposes in mind: speed and stealth. Comfort wasn't a priority. The stern was for the engines and fuel, and the bow was for their cargo. What space remained for the cockpit was barely larger than a phone booth.

Both men were sweating profusely in the hot, cramped space. The sounds of the engines were loud, making it difficult to think, let alone communicate. Both men were feeling the tension, the weight of the entire operation resting on their shoulders.

The middle-aged man reached into his pocket and pulled out a picture of his wife and daughter. He flipped it over and read the words *mi amor* handwritten on the back. He closed his eyes for a moment and looked down.

He'd never meant to lead the life he was living. Growing up in rural Panama, he'd been raised to be a coffee farmer. His parents had been killed by gang violence when he was young, and a life of crime had become his only means of survival. But this was it, he told himself. One final run; one last push into harm's way. Once it was over, he'd take his cut, return to his family and run away with them. He'd given the narcos twenty years of his life. He'd give them no more.

"Rodrigo!" the young man said suddenly over the loud rumbling engines. "There is an aircraft flying toward us."

The experienced drug runner leaned over the young man's shoulder and peered at the radar screen. The echo was moving fast and was only five miles north of their current position.

He squeezed his sweaty hands, tightening them into strong fists.

They'd already had to change plans thanks to a Coast Guard patrol boat blocking their approach to Miami. Rodrigo knew there was no way that they could motor past a Jayhawk helicopter without being seen. It was possible that it wasn't military, but the chances were slim. It was 0300. Not exactly a popular time for private pilots to fly about in the Gulf.

Rodrigo glanced at the speedometer. The row of

six 250-hp engines were rocketing them across the water at eighty knots, a daredevilish speed for a boat. He gazed at the fuel gauge and shook his head. The indicator was getting dangerously low. The boat had been throttling at full speed since leaving the Northern Yucatan nearly four hours earlier. Since that time, the engines had guzzled down more than five hundred gallons of fuel. They were running out of time.

Rodrigo grabbed his chart, hoping for some kind of miracle. He could hear the beeping echo as it came closer and closer. With the clock ticking down, he examined the nearby geography and quickly made a decision.

Grabbing the throttles, he eased back, bringing their speed all the way down to thirty knots.

"What are you doing, Rodrigo?" the young man said.

By way of an answer, Rodrigo turned the helm to the right, putting them on an easterly course.

"We're going upriver, Samar," he said. "Shark River," he added, reading the label on the chart.

They had no choice but to hide. Turning back out into the Gulf would be suicide. They'd be sitting ducks in a matter of minutes when their fuel ran out. No, their only hope would be to hide and make contact with their people in the States in order to orchestrate their recovery.

Rodrigo kept a sharp eye on their speed and depth. He pushed open the hatch and breathed in the fresh ocean air. Popping his head out, he navigated the sleek craft through the mouth of the river, keeping a sharp eye out for land and other boats. The drug-running craft rode low in the water, the topside having less than a foot of freeboard above the waterline.

A few miles up the tangle of waterways, he idled the engines and waited, their eyes locked on the passing echo. They both held their breath, and sweat coated their brows. They watched as the chopper skirted the edges of their radar. Both men let out a sigh of relief as the aircraft flew by, keeping to a straight course without deviating in their direction.

Rodrigo smiled, but only for a brief moment. He glanced over at the fuel gauge and shook his head. He didn't need to perform a calculation to know that they didn't have enough fuel to reach their new drop-off location near Chokoloskee Bay. If they tried to go for it, he knew that the engines would sputter, die off, and leave them stranded in the Gulf.

"What are we going to do now?" Samar asked apprehensively.

Rodrigo grabbed the chart again and examined it under the dim cockpit lights. He spotted an out-of-the-way inlet a quarter of a mile farther upriver. Rising up into the night air for a better view, he eased forward on the throttles and navigated the craft to their destination. When they reached the inlet, it was exactly how he'd hoped it would be: empty, quiet, and dark.

He killed the engines, and Samar tied them off to a few thick branches on the shore. It was humid and there were bugs everywhere, so they stayed inside and powered on a small portable fan. Rodrigo leaned back to get some sleep, but his mind wouldn't allow it. He checked his phone again—still no signal. They were stuck in the middle of nowhere.

He looked forward at a small wooden compartment door behind Samar. They had over a thousand pounds of cocaine loaded up into that boat.

At the going rate of seventy-five dollars per gram, that meant well over thirty million dollars' worth of product. But the white powder was worthless if they couldn't exchange it with their boys in the States.

After two hours of sitting quietly in the dark, trying to get ahold of the buyers on his phone, Rodrigo heard the distant humming of an engine. The two sat quietly and listened as the unwelcome sound grew louder and louder.

~ ~ ~

"Why are we stopping?" the man grunted.

He looked over his shoulder at the guy piloting the airboat.

"I see something," the man seated at the controls replied.

Both men were big and bulky. The pilot was bald; the guy up front had short black hair and burn scars covering much of his face. They were both dressed from head to toe in camouflage, and their faces were covered in dark paint.

Baldy strode over to the starboard gunwale for a better look. He was a hard, rough man, just like his companion. Down a narrow channel to his right, he spotted an object against the shore. It was big and dark. It just barely rose out of the water. Looked like a large floating log. But logs don't have engines, and this thing had a whole row of them clamped down to its stern.

"Holy shit," Baldy said.

He took a deep drag from the Marlboro in his mouth, then exhaled the smoke.

"You know what that is, Jeb?" he continued. "It's

a smuggling boat. I saw a picture once. Drug runners down in South America use them to bring illegal shit into the states."

The big guy with the burn scars looked over at the strange-looking boat and shrugged.

"So what? It don't affect us none. Let's get a move on."

"You don't got a lick of sense, do ya?" Baldy snarled. "We stumble on a fucking gold mine and you wanna tuck tail and run. The hell's the matter with you?"

The guys had been living off the grid and away from the eyes of the law as best they could for a few years. With their finances running low, they were in dire need of cash.

"Screw you, Buck," Jeb replied. "We don't even know if there's anything aboard."

Buck paused. A dark, sinister smile appeared on his face.

"Yeah, well, there's one way we can damn sure find out."

He snatched the silver Smith & Wesson revolver from his waistband and aimed it at the barely visible boat.

"We're going over there."

He sat back at the controls, started up the big engine, and accelerated them over toward the boat. Stealth wasn't an option in an airboat. If there were people still aboard, they'd have already heard them. So Buck had his revolver ready and Jeb had an arrow nocked and ready to draw back in his compound hunting bow.

Buck killed the engine when they were fifty feet away, letting them drift the remaining distance.

"It looks abandoned," Jeb said. "Been here for

God knows how long."

Buck shook his head.

"You idiot," he said. "Look at the paint. Look at the damn hull. No corrosion. This shit's new."

The two guys froze as they heard a sound coming from the stern of the boat. They both raised their weapons and watched as the rear hatch hinged open. Suddenly, Rodrigo's head popped out. He stared at the two intruders for a few seconds, his right hand gripping his custom Beretta M9.

"You lost or sumthin'?" Buck said, breaking the short, tension-filled silence.

Rodrigo didn't speak for a few seconds. He analyzed the two big guys, trying to figure out what kind of men they were.

"You know, if ya lost, we can help you," Buck continued. "Get you wherever it is you're lookin' to go."

Rodrigo eyed the guy skeptically. He got a bad vibe from them but wasn't exactly overwhelmed with options.

"Why would you help us?" Rodrigo said.

Buck raised his eyebrows slightly and gave a strange smile that put his nasty yellow teeth on full display. "Could be… mutually beneficial."

"How so?"

"We'll help you for a price."

Rodrigo shrugged. "We don't have money."

"No?" Buck said. "Well, you've got sumthin' on that boat of yours."

Rodrigo looked out over the water.

"We'll give you a pound for fuel," he said. "That's worth over thirty thousand dollars."

Buck laughed and shook his head. He exchanged glances with Jeb, then said, "We'll be needin' half of whatever you got in there."

Half? Rodrigo thought.

The idea was ridiculous. But he figured that they could off the two rednecks once they delivered the fuel they needed.

"Fine," Rodrigo said. "We need fuel. You deliver it to us here and we'll give you half."

Buck smiled. "Deal."

Rodrigo stepped out onto the deck with Samar right behind him. Holstering his Beretta, he stepped toward the airboat.

"On second thought," Buck said, stepping from the bow of the airboat onto the flat deck of the go-fast boat, "we'll be requiring the payment up front."

Rodrigo shifted his position. He was beginning to feel uncomfortable, not liking the turn their conversation had taken. He looked back and forth between the two guys. Buck was just a few feet in front of him, his massive frame towering over his own.

Seeing the sinister look on both of their faces, Rodrigo quickly drew his weapon. But he wasn't fast enough. Before he could level the cannon, a loud boom shook the sleepy night air as Buck raised his revolver and pulled the trigger.

Rodrigo's head and arms snapped forward as the .45-caliber hollow-point tore into his chest at over a thousand feet per second. The lead round mushroomed, flattening and blasting a hole out his back six inches wide. The momentum from the blow launched his body backward. Blood, cartilage, and shreds of his shirt flew out. His body tumbled over the side and he was dead before he splashed into the murky water.

Samar stood frozen in shock for a moment. He

stared down at the mangled, motionless body of his friend and mentor. His heart raced, his eyes snapped up, and he gave out a shrill cry.

A moment later, he lunged toward Buck with reckless abandon. The big guy smacked him across the face with the back of his hand, then shattered his left knee with a powerful kick of his boot. Samar fell hard to the mud and wailed in pain as he wrapped his hands around his broken joint. He tried to stand but couldn't. The pain was too intense.

"Shut that bitch up," Jeb said, jumping onto the go-fast boat alongside Buck.

Buck raised his revolver and pulled the trigger. The round blew Samar's face apart and blasted a massive hole out the back of his skull. He flew back and splashed into the water beside his mentor. Both big guys stood over the bodies, unfazed and unaffected.

"Let's get this shit loaded up," Buck said as he crawled down into the cockpit.

The bulky guys barely fit inside, having to shuffle sideways in order to reach a wooden door at the bulkhead. Breaking it open, Buck shined his flashlight inside. There were stacks of sealed plastic-wrapped packages rising from the deck all the way to the overhead. The entire space forward of the cockpit was filled with the illegal drug.

Buck froze for a moment. His mouth dropped open and he looked back at his companion.

"Holy mother of coke," Jeb said. "There's gotta be hundreds of pounds here."

Buck nodded and smiled. They went to work, creating a small assembly line. Buck hauled it up onto the deck while Jeb threw it into their airboat and stacked it. After half an hour, their boat was full and they'd barely made a dent in the haul.

As they were about to get the hell out of there, Jeb suggested that they cut the boat loose.

"All I'm saying is, when these druggies find out their products gone missin', they're gonna come lookin' for it. So I say we—"

"We send this thing packing downriver," Buck finished his sentence. "And we throw some of the coke into the water for good measure. They'll be real confused then."

"What about these two?" Jeb motioned toward the two dead guys floating facedown in the water.

"That's the beauty of livin' in the Glades. Got natural crime scene cleanup crews ready to go. I'll wager the gators will take them away before the sun's up."

Jeb laughed. "Wait till Dale sees what we got. Beats the hell outta just a hog."

They cut the lines, motored the drug-running boat out into the main section of Shark River, and let her go. The current was slower than molasses, but after a few days, she'd reach the Gulf. The two guys wagered that she'd be found much earlier than that and there'd be a big story. Meanwhile, they'd be long gone.

Buck sat back in the control seat and punched the throttles. In just a few short seconds, they were flying across the water, vanishing into the dark depths of the Glades.

ONE

Everglades National Park
August 2009

"There it is!" George exclaimed as he stared through his binoculars.

He pointed up ahead. About half a mile away from them was a small skiff tied off to a shore of mangroves. Their skiff.

"Oh, thank God," Rachel replied. She bent down to catch her breath and wiped a layer of sweat from her brow. "I thought we'd never find it."

Birdwatching was a favorite pastime of theirs, and they'd been swept up in the beauty and diversity that the Glades offered. It was understandable, considering that the unique landscape was home to over three hundred and sixty species of birds. The pair had ventured a little too far out into the swamps and had gotten lost.

"Time for some food, water, and a hot bath," Rachel said.

George and Rachel Shepherd were a retired couple who'd spent most of their lives in Boston. They migrated down to the Florida Keys after their children moved out and had fallen in love with the island lifestyle. After retiring a few years earlier, they'd sold their house and bought a forty-four-foot catamaran with plans of sailing it around the world. They'd moored in St. Petersburg to spend time with their new grandchild and had ended up spending much more time with family than they'd planned. Now, they were sailing down south and had stopped over for the day to explore the Everglades.

George glanced down at his watch and realized that they'd spent nearly four hours searching the never-ending swamp for their tied-off boat. They were both in their mid-fifties but were in great shape for their age. Regardless, hours trekking through thick swamp had taken a toll on their bodies. It was a good thing they'd found their boat when they had. The sun was barely a sliver on the horizon, and the air around them grew darker by the second.

He adjusted his backpack, which contained two empty water bottles, a few candy bar wrappers, bug spray, and two rolled-up rain ponchos.

"I'm sorry, Rach," he said.

"Hey, we both got lost," she replied. "Though I do usually count on your sense of direction."

They trekked through the mud, grass, and shallow water and reached their fourteen-foot Carolina center-console half an hour later. By the time they were untying the line, the sun was gone and the sky dark.

Rachel climbed aboard and sat on the middle bench. George coiled the line, then dropped it at the stern along with his backpack.

"You sure you can get us out of here, Magellan?" Rachel said.

George laughed. They still had to navigate across the eastern section of Whitewater Bay. Their catamaran was anchored in a deep inlet at the mouth of Little Shark River roughly eight miles away near Ponce de Leon Bay.

"No more hiccups," he replied.

Just as he was about to shove their boat into the water, he heard the distinct sound of voices. They were close, just down the shore. He turned and focused his eyes in the direction of the sounds, but couldn't see anything. Whoever it was, they were hidden behind a small cluster of cypress trees.

George stood still for a moment, listening intently. From that far away, all he could hear was muffled voices. He couldn't make out any distinct words, but it was clear that their conversation was growing heated.

"I'll be right back," he said.

The retired surgeon was curious by nature. Always had been. He figured he could stroll over, take a peek at what all the commotion was about, and skip right back over to the boat.

Rachel jumped out and strode over beside him.

"What's going on?" she said, hearing the voices as well.

"I don't know. But it doesn't sound good."

Rachel moved in front of her husband, placing a hand on his chest.

"And what exactly are we going to do?"

"They might need help, Rach," he said. "The least I can do is check and see what's going on."

Rachel lifted her hands and relented. The two moved quietly along the grassy shore. Moving across a small jut of cypress covered land, they took cover in the foliage and got their first glimpse of the scene. There were four guys in all. Two big fat guys dressed in camo and two hippie-looking guys. One of the big guys was bald and had a backpack slung over one shoulder. The other looked like he'd endured severe burns to his face. They were standing in a small clearing near the shore. Two boats rested behind them, an airboat and a sleek-looking powerboat.

George and Rachel kept quiet and listened carefully.

"You'll pay the agreed-upon price, or we'll take our business someplace else," one of the big guys said.

Both of the hippies laughed.

"Someplace else?" one of them replied. "Look around, you dumb redneck. No one else is buying out here."

The big bald guy threw a punch that landed the hippie on his ass. The other hippie guy jumped in, and a fight broke out. There were yells and grunts of pain. In the heat of the scuffle, the backpack over Baldy's shoulder was flung through the air. It landed in the shrubs and tumbled onto the ground less than ten feet away from where George and Rachel were hiding.

The main compartment of the backpack had ripped open. A handful of small plastic-wrapped packages fell out.

Rachel placed a hand on her husband's shoulder.

"We should leave, now!" she whispered into his ear.

George could hear the terror in his wife's voice. He agreed. Though he wanted to help if someone got hurt, they were in danger there. These guys were clearly all criminals, and tensions were high.

Before turning around, he moved forward, snatched the closest package, and slid it into his pocket. The big bald guy suddenly looked in his direction. For a brief moment, the two made eye contact before George turned around and took off. He kept low alongside Rachel and they moved quickly back toward their boat. Their hearts pounded violently as they ran with every ounce of energy they had left. When they reached the boat, they heard loud screams coming from behind them, capped off by a deafening gunshot that echoed across the swamp.

George helped his wife aboard, then shoved their boat into the water. Climbing up and sitting on the backseat, he started up the 90-hp Yamaha engine and turned sharply as he accelerated them into Whitewater Bay.

He saw me, George thought. *He looked right at me.*

He was breathing heavily and holding tight to the wheel. For a moment he felt a sense of relief as the engine propelled them both away from the scene.

Maybe he didn't see me. Maybe we were hidden by the branches and this is all just in my head.

As he motored along between two mangrove-covered islands, he heard a sound coming from behind them. It was loud and unnatural, and it was getting louder.

His heart sank deep into his chest. He looked over his shoulder and saw an airboat rocketing around the shore they'd just shoved off from. The engine boomed as it spun the propeller around in a frenzy, rocketing the craft straight toward them. It was far back, but he could see the outline of the two big guys aboard.

George snapped his head forward and gunned the

throttles. The engine groaned and accelerated them up to their max speed of thirty-five knots. Rachel stared back at the approaching boat, then dropped down and grabbed hold of the railing as they bounced up and down. The dark world flew by them in a blur as George maneuvered around island after island, motoring them closer and closer to their anchored catamaran.

As they entered Oyster Bay, he spotted something far out over the port bow. There was the dark silhouette of a simple shelter and a tied-off boat about a mile away. He thought he saw movement, but he couldn't be sure. It was too far away, too dark, and they were motoring too fast. He didn't have time to wonder who it might be or if they could help them. He kept his eyes forward and focused. Kept his hand tight around the wheel.

He looked back again to gauge their distance from their pursuers. Looked about half a mile, but it was difficult to tell in the dark. He didn't know how fast the airboat was but was confident that they could reach their catamaran before being overtaken.

But what then? They're still two armed criminals against us.

He had a compact Ruger 9mm handgun hidden away in the main stateroom of the cat. If they could make it, they'd have a chance. They also had a long-range radio in the cockpit of their anchored boat. They could at least send out a distress call.

Wind billowed violently against his face as he slid his phone from his pocket, verifying that there was still no signal. He shook his head, slid his phone back into his pocket, and piloted them as fast as he could. His eyes burned with resolution, and adrenaline surged through his veins. He'd been involved in life-or-death situations all his adult life. He'd pulled it together and saved the lives of countless people. Now it was time to focus and get himself and his wife out of there alive.

The sounds of the airboat grew louder behind them as they reached the end of Oyster Bay. George turned sharply, weaving in and out of a cluster of small islands before motoring them into Little Shark River. They were just a few miles from their destination, but with each glance over his shoulder, George saw that the airboat was quickly closing in on them.

The sounds of its engine and propeller were quickly overtaking the sounds of their own engine. He could also hear screams and shouts from low, angry male voices, cursing and threatening them violently.

"You're a dead man!" he heard one of the voices shout over the sounds of the engines.

As they came within a mile of their catamaran, the airboat closed to within a few hundred yards. A loud bang filled the air as something slammed against the transom. Both George and Rachel dropped as low as they could. It hadn't been a bullet. George knew that. It'd been too big to be a bullet.

He glanced back and saw an arrow sticking out inches from the top of the transom. He shifted his gaze back to the airboat and saw one of the big guys standing on the bow, aiming an arrow straight at them.

"Stay down!" George yelled as he dropped low, holding on to the wheel and piloting without looking.

A second bang resonated from the hull, followed a few moments later by a shattering of the small windshield as an arrow tore through the glass. They were being bombarded. Arrow after arrow slammed into their boat as the two attackers tried their best to stop them dead in their tracks.

Glancing up over the bow for an instant, George caught a glimpse of their boat. They were almost there, and they'd need to act quickly if they were going to get aboard and make any attempt at getting out of there alive. Soon arrows weren't their only concern. Their attackers started firing off bullets that rattled against the transom and zipped right over their heads.

One round struck the engine just as they reached their anchored boat. It smoked and sputtered, causing them to slow.

This is it. We have to move now, and we have to move fast!

George rose to his feet, strode as quickly as he could toward the bow, and practically tackled his wife over the edge and into the dark water. They swam as fast as they could, their hearts pounding and their lungs screaming for air. They reached the stern of the cat just as their attackers closed in. Bullets struck the fiberglass around them as they climbed up onto the swim platform.

George felt a sudden sharp pain radiate from his side, and he fell hard to the deck. He looked down and saw blood gushing out onto the white deck beside him. Rachel lunged over to her husband, but she was struck as well. She tumbled and slammed hard onto the port side of the stern. Her head struck the hard edge, knocking her unconscious.

George gasped for air. He could feel the life draining out of him with each passing second. Tears filled his eyes as he gazed upon his wife's unconscious body.

The two attackers motored right up to the swim platform. One of them hopped over casually and stood over George as he struggled to keep his eyes open. The big guy didn't hesitate. He didn't say a word or show any sign or remorse. He simply raised his revolver and finished both of them off with a succession of high-caliber rounds.

He held on to the smoking revolver and stared at their lifeless bodies for a few seconds. He felt nothing, no pang of guilt or wave of shame. This wasn't the first time they'd caught people snooping on their dealings. Even in the middle of nowhere, people occasionally saw things. And the men couldn't let anyone get away and tell the world what they'd seen. There was too much at stake.

"What we gonna do about the boat?" Jeb said from the airboat.

Buck turned and looked over his shoulder.

"We fucking burn it."

They punctured the catamaran's gas tank, spilling the flammable liquid all over the engine room. With a quick flick of a match, the boat caught fire. The small skiff was sinking due to the holes they'd put in its hull. It took less than a minute for it to disappear into the dark water alongside them.

"Been a long ass day," Jeb said as he climbed off the burning catamaran and onto their airboat. "Let's get back home before somebody sees the fire."

He turned to look at Buck who was stepping toward the control seat.

"We're not going home yet," he said.

"Why the hell not?"

"We have unfinished business." Jeb looked over in confusion, and Buck added, "We both saw that guy at the Oyster Bay Chickee. And worse, he saw us."

Jeb shook his head. "Ah shit, Buck. It's dark and he was far off. Probably didn't get a good look at us."

"He had an airboat," Buck replied. "He's most likely a hunter. You don't think there's a chance that he's got night vision? Besides, even in the dark he could see our boat in the moonlight. What have I always told you about loose ends, Jeb?"

Jeb didn't have to look at the two mangled bodies resting on the burning catamaran beside him to answer the question.

"I know, I know," he said. "We don't leave any."

Buck nodded, took one more look at the cat, then started up the airboat's engine and accelerated back in the direction they'd come, the catamaran exploding at their backs. Massive flames engulfed the vessel, lighting up the night sky for miles around.

When they reached the other side of Oyster Bay, the Chickee was empty. The man they'd seen while passing by had vanished, along with his boat.

"I don't care who you call," Buck turned to Jeb and snarled. "You figure out who that guy was." He paused a moment, then added, "I want his ass dead."

TWO

Three months after taking off from the turquoise waters of Curaçao, we picked up Ange's Cessna from the hangar in Miami and were on our way back to the Florida Keys. We'd loved and completely soaked in the globetrotting lifestyle. We were well rested, happy, and deeper in love than we'd ever been before. Part of us didn't want our trip to end, but we also missed our life back home. We missed our friends, our house, and we missed our dog, Atticus.

Ange brought us down into Tarpon Cove just a few days after a hurricane and a tropical storm both made close calls with the island chain. Hurricane Bill peaked as a category four but fortunately quieted down by the time it reached most of the Eastern Seaboard. Just a day after Bill died off, a tropical wave and an upper-level low-pressure system formed into Tropical Storm Claudette just south of Tallahassee. The storm killed two people due to rough seas and caused moderate rainfall across much of Florida but little damage.

My old friend Jack Rubio met us at the marina. He had his blue Wrangler parked in the lot and was standing alongside a very happy yellow Lab as we motored up to the fenders. His curly blond hair danced in the wind from the propeller as he grabbed hold of the wing brace. Once in position, Ange killed the engine.

"Mr. and Mrs. Dodge," Jack said as I rolled down my window. "Nice of you guys to stop by."

Ange and I exchanged one final honeymoon kiss before I opened my door, climbed down onto the starboard pontoon, and hopped over to the dock.

"It's good to see you, brother," I said, wrapping my arms around him.

Atticus, unable to contain his enthusiasm, shimmied his way in between us and jumped up and down.

"And it's good to see you too, boy," I said.

I knelt down and squeezed him tight for a second before loosening my grip and petting him while he licked my face with more excitement than a kid with an ice cream cone on a hot summer day.

Turning around, I offered a hand to Ange as she stepped onto the dock. She looked beautiful as usual, with her blond hair tied back and her sunglasses on. She was wearing a gray tank top and a pair of black shorts that made it difficult for me to keep my eyes off her long, tanned legs.

I tied off the Cessna, and after a brief moment of catching up, Jack helped us bring our bags down the dock and load them into the back of his Wrangler.

"You two had some of the locals worried," Jack said. "They thought you might never come back."

"The Keys are our home now," Ange said. "There's no place like it."

"But you should see Fiji," I said as we climbed into the back and he started the engine.

"I wanna hear all about it, bro," he said as he drove out of the parking lot.

Jack had the top down, and the tropical breeze felt good. We gave him a brief overview of our trip while he drove us over to our house on Palmetto Street. There was a lot to talk about, on both our ends. I looked forward to meeting up with him again later that day.

My house and property looked good as we pulled into the driveway. I'd paid Jack's nephew, Isaac, a few hundred bucks to mow the grass and take care of the plants while we were gone, and he'd done a good job.

Jack idled the engine just behind my black Tacoma 4x4. Sliding over to the side, we hopped out and grabbed our bags.

"Thanks for the lift," I said.

"Don't mention it. *Bullets* looks good, by the way," Jack said, referring to my 48 Baia Flash moored over at the Conch Harbor Marina. It'd been Jack's idea to call her *Dodging Bullets* when I'd bought her over a year earlier. "I had the oil changed last month. Engines are both purring like kittens."

"Thanks, Jack," I said. "You wanna do Pete's for dinner tonight?"

"Any other time and you know I would, compadre. But you two have other plans, remember?"

I looked at my old friend questioningly. Just as I opened my mouth to ask him what he was talking about, Ange stepped toward me and placed a hand on my shoulder.

"That's my fault, Logan," she said. "I forgot to tell you."

26

I raised my eyebrows and looked back and forth between them.

"You guys gonna keep me in the dark here?" I said with a smile.

"We're booked at a hotel tonight," Ange said. "Courtesy of Professor Frank Murchison."

I grinned and nodded. "Is it in Key West?"

"Key Largo," Ange said. "And I think you're really going to like it."

We said goodbye to Jack, then headed down a short footpath, with Atticus taking the lead. We lumbered up the stairs of our stilted house and entered through one of the side doors. I dropped my bags in the bedroom, then stepped out onto the balcony and took in a deep breath. It felt good to be back.

There's something about coming home after a long absence. It's a unique feeling, an experience that's both new and familiar. It's everything about it. The smells of the house, the sounds of birds and the wind through the surrounding palm leaves, the view of the channel through our living room window. And little things like the particular sound a door makes when you open it. Plopping your head down onto your own pillow. Dropping into your favorite spot on the couch.

Ange stepped out beside me, and I grabbed her softly by the hand.

"Welcome home, Mrs. Dodge," I said, pulling her in close.

We shared a long, warm shower. It felt good to wash off the sweat and stink from a day of travel. Once done, we each put on a fresh set of clothes, then packed a bag. We were only going away for one night, so we didn't need much. I was looking forward to sleeping in my own bed again but was also excited for whatever Ange and Frank had planned.

Once the truck was loaded up, we locked up the place and hopped onto US-1, heading east. It was a beautiful afternoon in paradise as we drove from one island to the next across my favorite stretch of pavement on earth. A hundred-mile drive of picturesque islands, quaint shops, and a horizon of blue surrounding us. With the mercury up over eighty degrees, we had the windows down and the radio blaring island favorites.

Just over two hours later, as the sun was tickling the horizon, we pulled into a parking spot at our destination. I looked around and saw no sign of anything resembling a hotel. Ange still hadn't said a word about where we were staying, so I leaned out the window and read the large white sign with blue letters.

"The Largo Undersea Hotel," I said.

Ange patted me on the shoulder. "It's the perfect place for an aquanaut like you."

I smiled. "This looks interesting."

After grabbing our bag, we headed inside to check in and settle into our room. The receptionist led us out back to a wharf alongside a calm lagoon filled with buoys and flanked on either end by docks. Peering over the edge, I spotted two submerged structures roughly twenty feet beneath the clear water's surface. I expected there to be a staircase that led down into the underwater structure. But instead of stairs, the receptionist led us into a large room filled with scuba equipment.

"You two ever dive before?" a guy wearing a white tee shirt with a red dive flag on it said.

"A few times," Ange replied with a grin.

Within minutes, we were changed and geared up,

with BCDs strapped over our bodies and air tanks on our backs. They even had a large plastic case to put our bag in for the journey down. I asked Ange what she'd planned to do with Atticus, but the diver, whose name we found out was Rick, provided a solution to that as well.

"No problem, man," he said. "My wife loves dogs, and we'll watch over him. We live right above the office, so he'll be here if you ever want to see him."

I thanked him, said a quick goodbye to Atticus by scratching under his ears, then Ange and I headed down a small set of concrete steps.

"Scuba diving down into a hotel room?" I said as I stepped toward the edge with my mask hanging around my neck and my fins in my left hand. "Now I've seen everything."

Once properly weighted, we donned our fins and stepped into the water. Venting the air from our BCDs, we descended to the bottom alongside Rick, who referred to himself as the bellhop. The water had a slight green hue to it, but the viz was good. We spotted a handful of tarpon and a large stone crab as we finned under the cube-shaped structure, then broke the surface through a square opening. After climbing up into the room and sliding out of our gear, I grabbed a towel and handed it to Ange.

"There's a welcome book in the galley that should answer any of your questions," Rick said from the water. He still had his mask on, so his voice was high-pitched. "Just give us a call to let us know what you want for dinner."

"Give you a call?" I said with raised eyebrows.

"Yeah," he replied with a smile. "We offer room service."

29

Ange and I dried off, changed, then relaxed in the living room. The room was small, probably just a few hundred square feet, but it had quite the view. Large portholes looked out into the ocean, allowing us to observe the various marine life from the comfort of our little home. I had to hand it to Frank, it was the most unique hotel I'd ever stayed at.

Less than an hour into our stay, Ange looked over the menu and decided on a big pepperoni pizza.

"Looks like dinner's here," Ange said half an hour later, pointing through the living room porthole.

I looked through and saw Rick swimming just a few feet from the glass. His right hand was waving at us and his left was clutching a yellow hardcase.

We strode over to the room we'd entered first, ducking our way through a small door. Rick rose up from the water and removed his mask.

"Pizza time," he said enthusiastically.

He unclasped the hardcase's hinges and opened it up, revealing the pizza. The smell filled the room and caused my mouth to water. We brought it back to the living room and ate the entire thing while we watched the fish swim by. It was delicious, and we washed it down with some fresh lemonade that had been left in the galley fridge.

A few hours later, I was just about to open a bottle of wine when I heard a sound coming from back in the entryway. Ange heard it too, and we both moved swiftly back into the small room. We arrived just in time to see another diver grab onto the edge of the hatch. I'd accumulated a long enough list of enemies in my life. It caused me to be cautious and always ready for the worst. But as I strode across the room, my eyes scanning for a potential weapon, the diver removed his mask.

"It's me," Jack said, letting the mask dangle under his chin and raising a hand.

"Jack?" I said, shaking my head. "What are you doing here?"

"Please tell me you're delivering us some Key lime pie," Ange said.

I smiled at Ange's remark, but my smile quickly died away when I saw the expression on my old friend's face. He was the most laid-back and carefree guy I'd ever met. But at that moment, he looked defeated, his eyes filled with despair.

"Hey," I said, kneeling down beside him. "Everything alright?"

He paused a moment, cleared his throat.

"You know that guy the papers used to call the Glades Killer?" he said.

His words caught me off guard. I hadn't heard mention of the famous Everglades serial killer in what felt like ages.

"I remember you telling me something about that," I said. "But that was years ago. They caught the guy, right?"

Jack shook his head. "No. And as far as I know, they've never been able to positively identify him."

He paused a moment, then climbed up out of the water and sat on the edge. He stared at the ground, water dripping from his hair.

"What happened, Jack?" Ange asked.

He took in a deep breath and let it all out. His solemn eyes trained up to meet mine.

"It's the Shepherds," he said.

His body was stoic, his tone grave. My heart raced at the mere mention of their last name. They were the retired couple I'd purchased the Baia from over a year earlier. They'd also saved my butt near

Cay Sal in the Bahamas after an intense firefight with a Russian mercenary. The last time I'd seen them was three months earlier, at our wedding on Curaçao.

"George and Rachel," Jack continued. "They were sailing their cat along the opening to Whitewater Bay, heading back down across the Caribbean." He paused a moment to clear his throat. "They're dead. They were murdered and their boat was set ablaze."

I sank down into a metal storage compartment as if a massive weight had just been dropped on top of me. My eyes widened and my head dropped. A strong resolution formed deep within me that quickly intensified into rage. I didn't know who the hell was responsible, but I knew one thing: I was going to find them, and I was going to rain brutal justice upon their doorstep.

THREE

Ange and I cut our stay at the Undersea Hotel short. We quickly loaded up our bag, donned our scuba gear, and finned back up to the surface. Rick met us on the edge, with Atticus standing right beside him and peering down at us eagerly. We didn't have the time or energy to explain what was going on. All we told Rick was that we had an emergency, and we thanked him for his hospitality as we changed.

Just a few minutes after exiting the water, we were hopping into my Tacoma. I glanced over at Ange as I fired up the engine. She was just as angry as I was and needed no convincing to drop everything and plan an unexpected trip to the Everglades.

I rolled down the window and told Jack we'd meet him at Pete's later that evening. He nodded, then climbed into his Wrangler and followed us as we drove down the side street and cruised onto US-1. Time was everything if we were going to figure out what had happened to the Shepherds. The colder a crime scene gets, the harder it is to figure out what happened. As we were donning our scuba gear, Jack had said that the incident had occurred the previous evening, which meant that we were already behind.

We kept quiet for most of the drive. I was deep in thought, and I could tell that Ange was as well. It was like a rotary switch inside me had instantly been turned from level one to ten. My mind was firing on all cylinders, thinking of everything we'd need and how we should go about the task of finding who was responsible.

As we cruised across the Seven Mile Bridge, Ange placed a hand on my knee.

"Hey," she said. "Are you okay?"

I relaxed a little and nodded. I couldn't get their faces out of my head. George had spent a career as a surgeon, while Rachel was a teacher. They were as innocent as could be, but someone had decided to kill them.

Why would anybody want to kill them?

I knew that if a serial killer was responsible, there wouldn't even need to be a motive. I'd read and watched enough about serial killers to know that they were sick, unstable human beings who often ended lives just for the hell of it.

It was just after 2200 when we pulled into the seashell lot in front of Salty Pete's Bar, Grill, and Museum. I parked along a wooden fence beside a gumbo-limbo tree and hopped out. From the outside, Pete's looked like a renovated old-style house. It was two stories, with a small porch with a door in front and a large balcony out back.

Atticus trotted over to his usual spot in the grass beside the door. Jack's headlights scanned over us as he pulled in, and he parked alongside my Tacoma.

"I called Pete." Jack stepped out and jogged over

to us. "He and a few other locals are upstairs waiting for us."

A bell rang as we entered. The place was dying off for the night. A handful of people at the bar and a few small groups in booths, but that was it. Clearly there was no live band playing that evening. If there was, there'd be a packed house.

"Hey, we're closing up the kitchen, the—" a man's voice said from back in the kitchen.

It was Osmond, Pete's massive Scandinavian cook. He was wearing his dirty white apron and had a towel over his left shoulder. His words trailed off as soon as he stepped out and laid eyes on us.

"Oh hey, guys," he said, stepping toward us. "You here for drinks? I could whip some food up too if you want."

"Not tonight, Oz," I said, motioning toward the staircase at the back of the room. "We're just here to see Pete."

Oz told us Pete was out on the balcony as we headed upstairs. The second story of the restaurant was the museum part, with rows of glass cases and various artifacts from around the Keys covering most of the floor space. We stepped out to the balcony through a sliding glass door and saw Pete look our way from the center table. He was in his early sixties and had a short, stocky build and a hook in lieu of a right hand. He ushered us over to the table where a few others were seated beside him. As we approached, I realized that it was Frank Murchison and Harper Ridley.

When we reached the table, Pete slid his chair back, rose slowly, and strode over to us. His hands were coated in a faint layer of grease, his tee shirt had black blotches all over it, and he had a dirty rag sticking out of the back pocket of his shorts. I remembered him mentioning a few weeks earlier that he was restoring his dad's '69 Camaro with a mechanic friend.

"Nice to have you back." He gave Ange and me both a big hug. "It's good to see you both. Though I wish I were seeing you tomorrow, and under different circumstances." His eyes glanced toward the floor, then darted back up. "You two must be hungry."

"Just two Key limeades will be fine," Ange said to Mia, who was standing beside the table.

The head waitress, a pretty woman in her early thirties, came over and gave Ange a hug before shuffling inside.

The four of us sat down, filling in all of the empty chairs around the table. Frank, a brilliant professor who'd migrated south to teach at Florida Keys Community College, kicked things off.

"Wasn't exactly the wedding present I had in mind," he said. He had an eloquent and articulate way of speaking that matched his style. "But at least you had three months to soak in some quality time."

"Thanks for the gift," I said.

"It really was a nice place," Ange added. "Even if we only had a few hours to enjoy it."

I nodded, scanning around the group. "Right now we have other business to attend to."

Mia came over and filled two glasses with Key limeade. I turned to look at Jack.

"You mentioned that serial killer—why? What makes you think he was involved?"

Jack shrugged. "I don't know for certain. But Mitch Ross was the one who called me. He was the first guy on scene, arrived just before the Coast Guard did. He's the head park ranger in the Everglades. He

36

said there didn't appear to be much to go on but that it looked like the work of the notorious killer."

"How long has it been since he murdered someone?" I asked incredulously. "I haven't read anything about him for years."

"Tough to say," Jack said.

"People go missing in the Glades," Pete added. "Over a million people come from all over the world to visit those swamps every year. A small number never leave. It can be a very dangerous and unforgiving place, due to its nature. But I'm sure this predator has kept busy over the years."

I leaned back into my chair, wrapped my hand around my chilled glass, and took a few sips of the delicious concoction.

"So, let me get this straight," Ange said. "This well-known killer has been murdering people in the Glades for years and no one's been able to do anything about it?"

There was a short pause.

"They've tried," Pete said. "Back in '03, local authorities mounted one of the largest search parties in Florida history. They numbered over fifty strong, and they were all well-armed. These weren't city cops either. These guys knew the swamps and they knew how to hunt."

"Not well enough, I guess," Ange said. "They find any clues at least?"

Pete shook his head. "Not that I know of. Though a Seminole Indian friend of mine was part of the search. He told me the killer was more of a spirit than a man. That he moved with the wind, seemingly disappearing at times and reappearing someplace else."

The table fell silent for a few seconds. Pete's

words didn't sway my resolve in the slightest. I'd dealt with cold-blooded, hard-nosed, highly trained killers for much of my life. Somebody had to do something, and I was never one to back down from a challenge.

"A spirit, huh?" I said. "Well, I guess I'll have to see about that."

"We're gonna have to see about that," Ange corrected me.

Pete nodded solemnly. His eyes scanned back and forth between us, then trained on Jack.

"They'll need you too," Pete said. "You know the swamps, Jack. And I'll call my Seminole friend. See if he can offer any assistance. You're a tough trio, not saying otherwise. But you guys are gonna need all the help you can get."

I killed the rest of my Key limeade, then glanced over at Harper. Harper Ridley was a reporter for the *Keynoter*, a local newspaper. She looked younger than her forty years and had been silent since we'd arrived. But she'd been hanging on every word and made a few notes on a notepad in front of her. I'd known her for years and trusted her, but it was surprising for her to be there.

"Don't take this the wrong way, Harper," I said, "but what exactly are you doing here? This is a private matter and shouldn't be in the paper."

"I called her," Pete said. "Asked her to come by."

I scratched my head.

"Why would you—"

"Because I have *this*, Logan," she said, cutting me off. She reached into her satchel and pulled out a photograph.

She handed it to me over the table. It was worn and the image was faded. I looked closer and saw that it was a picture of a swamp and that there was a human figure in the corner. The person was far away, his back to the camera, and most of his body was covered by tall sawgrass.

"So far as I know, that's the only picture ever taken of this guy," Harper said. "And this," she added, grabbing a small stack of papers from her satchel, "is a record of the various incidents surrounding him."

I grabbed the papers and riffled through them.

"These span over ten years," Ange said, leaning over the table in front of me.

Harper nodded. "It's believed that he's responsible for nine murders in that time. But, as Pete said, a lot of people go missing in the Glades. The actual number could be a lot higher."

"Is there any correlation between these murders?" I said. "Any hint as to what his motive might be?"

"Not really," Harper said. "Other than the fact that all of his victims were in the Glades. But usually, the incidents occur where the Watson River enters into Whitewater Bay."

I shot her a confused look. I'd been to the Glades a few times, but I didn't exactly know the place well.

"I got you covered, bro," Jack said. He rose to his feet and headed for the sliding glass door. "Pete, you still keep your charts in your office closet?"

Pete nodded, then spewed out the chart number and its orientation in a stack. A few seconds later, Jack returned with a cardboard tube. Popping the small plastic lid, he pulled out the chart, unrolled it, and flattened it onto the table using empty glasses.

"Watson River is here, bro," Jack said, pointing to the top-center of a chart that included the southern tip of mainland Florida, Whitewater Bay, and Florida Bay.

"There have been incidents all around that area," Harper said, leaning over the table.

"But the Shepherds were killed roughly eight miles west of there in Ponce de Leon Bay," Jack said, pointing at the chart.

"Could be this killer," Ange said. "Could be some other scumbag."

Pete nodded. "The Glades have attracted criminals and poachers for years. You should hear some of the stories the real old-timers tell of that place before it became a national park in '47. Place was a haven for Gladesmen, also known as swamp rats. They weren't all bad, of course. But they were a different breed of men than you see these days."

I nodded, grabbed the picture and the stack of papers, and rose to my feet.

"Harper, this conversation was off the record," I said.

She placed her right thumb and index finger to her mouth and slid them across her lips.

"My lips are sealed," she said, "in this matter at least. I'm just here to do what I can to help."

"So, what's the plan, bro?" Jack said.

I shrugged. "We head out in the morning. The crime scene's getting colder by the second."

"You taking the Baia?" Pete asked.

"We'll take the Cessna. The faster we get there, the better."

"Alright," he replied. "Then I'll take my boat and meet you guys there. Set up some kind of home base to offer support."

"Do me a favor and take the Baia, will you?" I said. "I can leave Atticus aboard in the morning and

40

leave the keys in the office."

Pete nodded.

Jack rolled up the chart and slid it back into the cardboard tube. Ange finished her drink and rose to her feet as well.

"We've got an early morning," I said, nodding to both Frank and Harper.

"You're back for less than twenty-four hours and now you're leaving again," Pete said, shaking his head. "Thought you might at least catch your breath before going off on another adventure."

"Didn't exactly choose this," I said. "And I caught my breath enough over the past three months."

Before the three of us reached the door, Pete walked over and stopped us.

"If you're gonna go after this guy, you need to be prepared," Pete said. "Whoever the hell he is, he's been living in the Glades for years. Never been caught. Never left a trace after a kill. He knows the swamps and he's comfortable there. The Glades are an unforgiving landscape. It's nearly eight thousand square miles of some of the harshest terrain in the country." He looked down at the deck. Cleared his throat. "Just be careful, and don't underestimate this predator."

FOUR

It was nearly midnight by the time we pulled into the driveway of our house over on Palmetto Street. It had been a long day, and Ange and I were eager to get a few hours of much-needed sleep before jetting off in search of justice. We crashed on the master bed with Atticus at our feet. Fatigue hit me hard, but it took a few minutes for me to fall asleep after my head hit the pillow. I had a difficult time driving the thought of the Shepherds from my mind.

My alarm woke me up well before the sun. I slapped it off, blinked a few times, and saw that it was 0400. My mind and body were hazy as I rolled out of bed, but I quickly shook it off. Four hours of sleep was more than enough. I'd been forced to perform at my best on much less over the course of my life.

Sensing my movement, Atticus looked up at me and tilted his head.

"Yeah, that's all we get tonight, boy," I said quietly.

I moved into the closet, shut the door behind me, and flipped on a light. Opening my biometric safe, I grabbed a few necessities, including an extra Sig Sauer P226 9mm pistol, my handgun of choice since my early days in the Navy. I also grabbed my M4A1 assault rifle, a Winchester 1300 shotgun along with a box of number four buckshot, primarily to take down pythons, and a small wad of cash.

The door opened behind me. I glanced over my shoulder and saw Ange step into view.

"Don't forget my sniper," she said.

I nodded, grabbing her collapsible .338 Lapua sniper rifle along with an extra magazine, then locked the safe up. Resting on a dresser in the closet was my black waterproof backpack that contained various essentials I'd gathered over the years. I grabbed it, and we also filled a few duffle bags with extra clothes, boots, hats, rain gear, sunglasses, MREs, bug spray, and various other items.

Ange reminded me that the gift my old Navy buddy, Scott Cooper, had given me was on the kitchen counter. It was a brand new top-of-the-line surveillance drone. We both figured that it would come in handy during a search of the Glades, so we grabbed the black hardcase and set it beside the rest of our gear.

After a quick shower, I dressed in a pair of cargo shorts, a Salty Pete's tee shirt, and my black sneakers. Ange whipped up a mango-banana smoothie and packed a few sandwiches into a small cooler as I loaded everything into my Tacoma. Once everything was set, I locked up the place and the three of us cruised out of the driveway.

Jack was waiting for us at the edge of the parking lot over at the Conch Harbor Marina when we pulled in. He was standing beside a large cart filled with dive equipment. I hopped out and gave him a hand loading his weights, fins, wetsuit, mask, and dive flashlights into the truck. I'd told him the night before that I'd wanted to start off the day by freediving the site where the Shepherds' catamaran had sunk.

I kept the truck idling and made a quick trip down the dock to slip twenty-four, where I kept *Dodging Bullets* moored. After grabbing Ange's and my gear, I locked it up and turned the security system back on. I left our scuba and rebreather gear aboard the Baia, figuring that if we needed it, Pete would have her moored at the southern part of the Glades in a few hours.

Gear in hand, Ange and I headed over to the marina office. Gus Henderson, the owner, was just stepping out of the main door when we walked by.

"Little early, isn't it?" Gus asked.

He was wearing pajamas and rubbed his dreary eyes.

"Give these to Pete," I said, handing him the keys to the Baia. "And top off the fuel for me, will you?"

He nodded. "Good to have you back. Heard about the Shepherds. Damn shame. And heard they don't even know who did it."

"For now," I said. "Oh, and Atticus is below deck on the Baia. Got the windows cracked and his bowls filled. Pete should be here soon, so no need to walk him."

Gus nodded.

I thanked him, and the three of us headed up the dock, dropped our gear into the back of my truck, then hopped in. We drove over to Tarpon Cove Marina and loaded everything into Ange's Cessna. She'd owned the 182 Skylane for four years and had been flying since she was a teenager. She'd convinced me to get my pilot's license a few years back but was still much better than I was, so she usually piloted.

Her bird was outfitted with two large floats that had forward and aft storage compartments. We loaded most of the dive gear into the floats, distributing them evenly, then hauled the rest into the back seat. Jack squeezed into the back, and I plopped down in the copilot's seat beside Ange.

She efficiently ran through all of the preflight checks while I performed verifications from the copilot seat. Once ready, Ange called in and got the all clear from air traffic controllers at Key West International Airport. I hopped out, untied the lines, then shoved the port pontoon away from the dock.

"All set," I said, climbing back into the cockpit and buckling my seat belt.

With the sky and ocean just outside the cove clear, she started up the 230-hp engine and accelerated us away from the dock.

It was a calm, eerie morning out on the water. The sky was dark, would be for a few more hours. The only light came from the silver glow of the waxing crescent moon that managed to radiate through patches of clouds.

Keeping a thorough eye on the surrounding water, Ange accelerated us up on plane at just over twenty-seven knots. With the floats in a planing attitude, the water supplied little resistance and she was able to accelerate us into a smooth takeoff.

We rose quickly above the dark tropical landscape. Ange banked steadily, making an arc over Dredgers Key and putting us on a northeasterly course. We flew over the hundreds of sporadic islands that make up the Great White Heron National Wildlife Refuge as Ange brought us up to our cruising altitude of twelve thousand feet.

Just under thirty minutes later, we finished the sixty-mile jump across the Gulf and reached the Florida mainland. The sun was just peeking over the eastern horizon as we flew over the southern tip of the Everglades. The sky was mostly devoid of clouds, allowing us to look out over the seemingly never-ending expanse of untamed swamps.

The killer is somewhere down there, I thought.

From a distance, the task seemed nearly impossible. It was easy to see how a man who knew the swamps could stay hidden in such a place. He had the terrain to his advantage, and it was obvious that he utilized it.

During the flight, Jack gave me the phone number for the head park ranger in the Everglades and I gave him a call using my sat phone. It would've been nearly impossible to hear anything over the sound of the Cessna's roaring engine, so I unplugged my headset from the dash and connected it to my sat phone.

It was my first time talking to Mitch, but it was clear within a few seconds that he was a smart guy. He gave me the location where the Shepherds' catamaran had sunk and let me know that we'd probably run into a detective or two if we went sniffing around the scene.

Before hanging up, I asked him if there were any leads so far.

"It's pretty barren in that regard," Mitch said in a smooth Southern drawl. "But there is one thing. A local claims to have seen something suspicious the night it happened. Said he saw two boats flying out of

Whitewater just after sunset. Said he heard gunshots, too."

"Who is he?"

"Don't know," Mitch replied. "Guy didn't give his name. We checked the reservations and Oyster Bay was supposed to be vacant that night. He called the morning after, during all of the helicopter commotion. He also said he saw the smoke."

"Smoke?"

"The cat was set ablaze after the two folks were killed. Not much left at the scene. Even the bodies were charred to the bones."

I paused a moment and swallowed.

"Any idea where I can find this guy?"

"No clue. But judging by his description, he was most likely staying at Oyster Bay Chickee when it happened." He paused a moment and cleared his throat. "I want you to know, Logan, that I'm not in the habit of giving out information like this to people I've never met before. But I want this guy gone bad, and both Pete and Jack speak very highly of you. If I can be of any further help with your search, you know how to reach me."

"Thanks, Mitch," I said.

We ended the call and I connected my headset back into the dashboard. I relayed to the others what Mitch had said. There wasn't much to go on, but we'd learn more once we were able to check out the scene.

At 0700, we splashed down in Ponce de Leon Bay on the western part of the Everglades. Ange had little trouble landing on choppy water, so the splashdown was smooth over the glassy bay. She kept the engine running, putting us on a southerly course with the edge of the Glades off the port side.

"That's Shark River Island," Jack said into the

headset, pointing to a mangrove-infested patch of land to the left. "Just around the corner we'll run into the mouth of Little Shark River."

"That's where the cat sank, right?" Ange asked.

Jack nodded. "Mitch told me the wreck is just a few hundred yards up river."

Ange motored us around the tip of the island, then turned west, heading into the wide opening of the river. It's called a river, but it's really more of a channel, as the water appears to stand still, moving imperceptibly slowly and shifting with the tides. Even that early, we'd spotted a few boats in the Gulf, but none were close to us as we headed toward the site of the wreck.

"Almost there," Jack said.

He was sitting in the back and had a chart opened up and a small GPS in his hand.

Ange brought us into a small cove, and I decided that it was time to get wet. Grabbing one of my bags from the back, I snatched my fins, mask, and snorkel. Then I pulled off my tee shirt, removed my shoes, and opened the starboard door.

"I'm gonna hold on to the pontoon and scan underwater as we move," I said. "I'll raise my hand and give a thumbs-up if I see anything." Ange and Jack both nodded, and I added, "How deep is it here, Jack?"

"Looking at around twelve feet according to the chart," he said. "But it varies, bro."

I looked back at him with raised eyebrows. Most of the waters in and around the southern part of the Glades maxed out at around five feet.

"I know," Jack said. "This whole little river is uncharacteristically deep."

I looked over through the open door at the water

below. With all the sediment washed up from the constant coming and going of the tide, the visibility would be terrible. But I figured it would be hard to miss a forty-four-foot catamaran.

"They don't call it Shark River for nothing, bro. It's filled with bulls."

Bull sharks are one of the few sharks that are known to attack humans. Known to be very aggressive, they also hold the distinction of being the only sharks able to live in both fresh and saltwater. The biggest adult females can reach over eleven feet long and weigh over five hundred pounds. Many experts consider bulls to be the most dangerous sharks in the world.

"If one takes a bite, you'll be the first to know about it," I said.

The saying that predators can sense your fear is true. It's not that these creatures can read your mind, but they can read and sense your body language. If you're afraid, your pulse and breathing will quicken, and your movements usually become jerkier. A shark or other apex predator can sense those changes in vibrations. For them, it's like the ringing of a cowbell letting them know that it's feeding time. The most important thing is to remain calm and focused.

I dangled my mask with the snorkel attached around my neck, grabbed my fins, and stepped down onto the starboard pontoon. After shutting the door behind me, I took a quick look around, hoping to catch a glimpse of something out of the ordinary. The Shepherds' cat had a mast that rose seventy feet into the air, but as I looked around, I couldn't see anything piercing the surface.

I moved back, sat on the edge of the pontoon as the water sloshed slowly beneath me, then donned my gear and dropped down into the water. It was warm but murky, so much so that I couldn't see more than a few feet, let alone the bottom. I gripped the pontoon tail rudder with my left hand and streamlined my body, the Cessna dragging me along. Using the snorkel, I breathed calmly in and out and scanned back and forth, hoping something would catch my eye.

After a few minutes, I felt the rudder twist and kicked my fins to relieve pressure on it as Ange turned the Cessna around, going for another pass. Less than a hundred feet into the second run, I spotted something in the corner of my eye. It was white and formed a right angle, something you don't see in nature. I raised my right hand high over my head and waved back and forth, signaling for Ange to stop. As the engine slowed, I took in a deep breath, let go, and dove down toward the object. After just a few kicks of my fins, it was clear that we'd stumbled upon the catamaran. Or at least what was left of it.

I swam over the charred pontoons and the main deck, which was disfigured, broken, melted, and black. It bore little resemblance to the beautiful boat I'd sailed from Cay Sal to Key West earlier that year. Being a sailing vessel, *Seas the Day* wouldn't have had very much fuel aboard. It was clear just from my initial survey that somebody must've spread fuel all over the boat to cause such damage.

After two minutes down looking for clues, I kicked up and broke the surface. Ange had killed the Cessna's engine and was floating fifty feet to the right of me, drifting slowly toward the Gulf.

"You find it?" Ange said, leaning out the pilot side window.

I nodded. "It's burned to hell." I glanced over at

a few thick mangrove branches two hundred feet or so behind the Cessna. "Let's tie off the bird."

After securing the plane, Ange and Jack donned their gear as well and joined me in the water. We spent half an hour surveying the wreck, looking for clues. While swimming off the stern along the mucky bottom, I spotted an object and kicked toward it. Moving just over the bottom, I spooked a large flounder that appeared from the sediment and darted away from me in an instant. It was probably the tenth one I'd seen, not surprising since the flat fish love hanging out at the mouths of rivers.

As I continued to kick, I realized that the object I'd spotted was an upside-down dinghy. The bow of the small boat was facing me and the engine was still attached, sticking up into the water with a handful of sticks pressed against it, carried there by the slow-moving current.

As I finned closer, I realized that they weren't sticks. They were arrows, three of them sticking all the way through the transom. They had broadhead tips, three razor-sharp blades that angled together to form a deadly point. As I observed the transom closer, I noticed bullet holes as well.

I kicked for the surface, then called over to the others. They dove down alongside me, and the three of us lifted the dinghy and turned it over. On first glance, it looked like there was nothing aboard, but Ange found a small object wedged under the middle bench seat.

I swam beside her and we both examined what she'd found. It was small, roughly the size of an eyeglass case, and wrapped in tight black plastic. She handed it to me and I was surprised by how soft it was.

My curiosity taking over, I grabbed my dive knife and poked a tiny hole through the plastic. Ange shined her underwater flashlight, and a small white cloud rose up from the hole I'd punctured. Jack was there now as well, and the three of us stared at the cloud with wide eyes. Each of us knew in an instant what it was. Cocaine.

Suddenly, we heard the unmistakable low hum of an approaching engine.

FIVE

Ange grabbed the package from my hand and pocketed it. Staying underwater, we swam toward the Cessna and rose up alongside its port pontoon. The three of us were experienced freedivers, able to stay down for minutes at a time and cover good distances on a single breath. As we rose up out of the water, our eyes darted toward the source of the engine sounds. Jack had told me that Little Shark River was routinely frequented by fishermen, but we wanted to be prepared for the worst.

Ange climbed up first, grabbed her Glock 19 from the cockpit, and held it at her side. Jack and I sat on the pontoon, our eyes peeled toward the opening of the river. The silhouette of a boat was cruising our direction at the mouth of the river less than a quarter of a mile away.

"Police boat," Ange said, her eyes peering through a pair of binoculars.

She set her Glock on the pilot's seat, then hid the

cocaine she'd found under the seat, grabbed a towel, and dried off her face before handing it to me.

A white center-console pulled up to us. The words on its hull indicated that it was a Monroe County Sheriff boat from the Islamorada District. There were two men aboard. Both wore white police polo shirts, black ball caps, and sunglasses. As it motored closer, I noticed a pair of rumbling Mercury 200-hp engines mounted to the stern.

One of the guys stepped up to the bow and stared at us with his hands on his hips as the other guy brought them right alongside us.

"What's going on here?" the guy at the bow asked.

His voice was higher pitched than I'd expected. He looked to be in his forties and had the gut of a guy who probably spent more time behind a desk than outside.

"Looking over the wreckage," I said flatly.

He tilted his head down, eyed me over the top of his sunglasses.

"This is a crime scene. You'll have to dive some other wreck. And if I figure out you've stolen anything, I'll—"

"We're not thieves, man," Jack said. "We knew the deceased. We're trying to track down who did this."

The guy sighed.

"It doesn't work like that," he said, raising his voice. "I'm the detective here, and the authorities will be the ones to track down whoever's responsible."

Ange laughed and shook her head. The guy's head snapped to look at her.

"Something funny, ma'am?"

"Yeah," she replied. "This guy's been killing

54

people for years and you've failed to catch him."

The man was visibly offended, but he quickly composed himself.

"There isn't sufficient evidence to make conclusions at this point," he said. "We don't know who's responsible, but we do know that it is our job to handle this, not yours."

I stood up on the pontoon and raised a hand.

"We're not trying to infringe," I said. "We're trying to help. What have you figured out so far?"

The guy stepped against the boat's starboard gunwale and slid off his sunglasses. His eyes were staring intently at me.

"Who are you?" he asked.

"Logan Dodge."

He paused a moment, then removed his sunglasses and looked me up and down.

"Charles told me about you," he said, his tone no longer agitated. "I was sorry to hear of his passing. He was a fine lawman."

"One of the best," I said. "And this is my wife, Angelina, and my friend, Jack Rubio."

Sheriff Charles Wilkes of the Key West Police Department had been a close friend of mine before he'd been murdered by corrupt members of a private military four months earlier.

"I'm Detective Milton," he said. He sighed and added, "Truth is there isn't much here. Most everything's been burned, as I'm sure you've already seen."

"Where are the bodies?" Ange asked.

"They were recovered early yesterday and taken to the Monroe County medical examiner." He paused a moment, looking out over the water. "I've seen some grotesque things in my time, but..." He cleared his throat. "There wasn't much left of them."

"Any word from the ME yet?" I asked.

"Aside from the severe burns, he said they each had a few gunshot wounds. And the guy had a broadhead burrowed in his side. The arrow burned away, but the tip was still intact." He looked down at the water. "You guys find anything?"

I made quick eye contact with Ange, then looked back at the detective.

"Found a dinghy," I said. "Had a few arrows lodged in the transom, but that's about it. It's murky as hell down there, tough to see anything."

Milton nodded. "Our diver had that same problem yesterday."

We talked for a few more minutes, then told him that we had plans to meet a friend of ours over at the Flamingo Visitor Center. He told us to inform him if we discovered anything else, and I lied and told him we would. I respect what they do as keepers of the peace, but as far as I was concerned, they'd had their shot. It was time for us to take ours.

We stowed our gear, untied the line, loaded up, and gave a quick wave through the windows as Ange fired up the engine and accelerated us up off the water.

"You didn't tell him about the coke, bro," Jack said into the headset.

"He didn't know the Shepherds like we did," I said. "The last thing I want is him suspecting they might be drug dealers or something."

Ange pulled back on the yoke, and we quickly gained altitude.

As she started to bank us around to the south, I said, "Let's swing by that place where the guy spotted the two boats."

56

"Oyster Bay Chickee?" Jack said.

"That's the one."

"It's east of here," Jack said. "Just over those islands. Probably five miles or so."

Ange nodded, straightened the controls, then eased us all the way around so that we were facing the rising sun. Jack grabbed the rolled-up chart and took a look.

Ange brought us down as Jack pointed through the windshield at a tiny dock resting just off the leeward side of a narrow island. Keeping an eye out for kayakers and airboats, Ange brought us down softly and motored us around the island. It appeared as though nobody was home as we looked around the channel and the "chickee" in front of us.

Chickee is the Seminole word for house, and today it's used to describe a rustic dwelling with a log frame and a raised floor. The Everglades are littered with the simple structures, which are essentially a dock with a roof and a porta potty. The National Park Service allows you to reserve a space on a chickee for the night, and I'd set up camp on them a few times during python-hunting trips.

I felt somewhat dejected as Ange killed the engine and I hopped out to tie us off. Though I knew it was unlikely that whoever had called in would still be around, it would've made tracking them down a hell of a lot easier.

The three of us caught our breath as we took a look around. It was perfectly quiet aside from the soft breeze through the mangroves and the water lapping against the cypress frame. A flock of sanderlings flew by, their wings flapping just a few inches above the water's surface. I'd read once that over four hundred species of birds live in the Everglades and that it's the most significant breeding ground for wading birds in North America.

A great egret stood in the shallows just a few feet from an overgrown bank across the channel, and off in the distance I could see the dark outline of a crocodile sunbathing on a muddy bank. The edges where the Glades meet the Gulf and Florida Bay are the only places in the States where you'll find crocs.

The place was teeming with life, just no human life. I stood on the edge and looked out over the water, imagining two boats flying by in the dark. George and Rachel on one, running for their lives. An unknown murderer on the other.

"You know, I've been thinking about those arrows in the dinghy," Jack said. "I don't know a lot about bows, but for an arrow that size to puncture an aluminum hull, I'd say it had to have been traveling well over three hundred feet per second."

"Must've been a nice bow," I said. "Probably a seventy-pound draw to do damage like that. Maybe more."

"Right," Jack said. "So how does a guy shoot a bow like that three times while piloting an airboat?"

I smiled and nodded, wondering why I hadn't thought of it.

"So, there was more than one guy."

"It's the only explanation," Jack said.

Great, I thought. *Now we're going after two murderers.*

"Well, what's the plan now, bro?" Jack said after a few seconds. "Time to head over to Flamingo?"

I nodded and took in a deep breath of fresh air.

"Anybody need to use the head before we leave?" I asked, motioning toward the bright blue porta potty.

58

Jack laughed. "Wouldn't go in one of those unless I absolutely had to. I can hold it."

I smiled. "Ange?"

When she didn't reply, I turned around and spotted her standing on the other side of the chickee. She was staring intently at the floorboards and the base of one of the side beams.

"Ange, you find something?" I said, striding over the planks toward her.

"Maybe," she said, keeping her eyes trained down. "Check these out."

I moved in close with Jack right on my heels. Ange pointed along a few of the planks.

"There are names carved into the wood," she said. "And dates."

I smiled and nodded. "Good eye. Nice to see that at least one of us is good at this."

There looked to be nearly a hundred carvings and most of them were worn and faded to the point of illegibility. But the most recent ones were readable.

"Here," Jack said, pointing halfway up the support beam. Ange and I rose and examined the wood. "T-J-S," Jack read the barely legible letters out loud, "Eight nineteen through…"

Even though the wood looked like it had been freshly cut, it was one of the hardest to read.

"Looks like he carved it away," I said. "Or at least he tried to. He must have decided last-minute that he didn't want anyone knowing that he was here."

"Or when he was here," Ange said. "He didn't write the day he left like all these other people did."

"Yesterday was the twentieth," I said. "Must be our guy."

I strode over to the Cessna, grabbed my sat

phone from inside, and dialed Mitch's number. He picked up on the third ring.

"Might have a fix on the caller," I said. "Initials T-J-S ring any bells?"

The ranger paused a moment.

"Teagan Suggs," he replied. "Shit, wish I'd taken that call. I'd have been able to tell it was him right away. His voice is raspier than a career coal miner's. Probably burns two packs a day."

"Any idea where we can find him?"

Mitch paused again.

"He's retired. Lives in Homestead, I think, and sometimes spends weeks out in the thick of it. Far as I know, his truck's still here, so he's somewhere out there. Wish I could be more specific than—"

He cut himself off mid-sentence. I heard a few muffled words as he brought the receiver away from his mouth and spoke to someone else.

A few seconds later, he said, "Logan, you still there?" After I told him I was, he added, "Martha here says that she saw Suggs over near Hells Bay half an hour ago."

He gave me a quick description of the guy— about six feet tall, heavyset, with a dark beard, medium-length hair and a silver earring in his left ear. He also said that he'd be cruising around in a Cottonmouth airboat that was painted dark green with a silver lightning bolt across each side.

"Oh, and if you find him, call him TJ," Mitch said. "His first name's a sore spot for him."

I thanked him and hung up.

"Well?" Jack said, raising his eyebrows at me.

"Looks like we've got a trail," I said. I stepped over to Ange, wrapped an arm around her and kissed her on the cheek. "Thanks to Nancy Drew here."

60

SIX

Soaring over thirteen miles of marshy landscape, we reached the eastern side of Whitewater Bay in well under ten minutes. Ange lowered us to just a few hundred feet when we reached Hells Bay and swept into a wide turn so we could get a better look. I peeked through the window and scanned the seemingly never-ending patches of green dotting the water beneath us.

We spotted an airboat at the northern section of the bay but turned back when we flew close and realized that it wasn't dark green and didn't have the silver lightning bolt Mitch had mentioned. As Ange turned, I saw a guy standing on the shore near the airboat. He was far away, but it looked like he was waving a fist in the air at us.

"Another one up ahead," Ange said, pointing through the windshield.

As we soared over the second boat, it was clear that we'd found a match. The boat was tied off in a small channel, and there was a guy wading in the water a few hundred yards south of it.

"Looks like a lightning bolt to me," Jack said through the headset.

He was leaning and peering through the port back window.

Ange brought us back around, then landed in the middle of the channel, motoring to a stop beside the airboat. The guy in the water looked over and stared as she killed the engine.

"I'll be right back," I said, hopping out of the cockpit and splashing into the waist-deep water.

Ange opened her door and leaned out as I sloshed around the tail, heading for the guy who Mitch said was Teagan Suggs.

"We'll be right here," she said, eyeing the guy across the channel.

"I'm sure we can scratch off this guy as being the killer," I said. "He probably wouldn't have called himself in."

She smiled and nodded.

I moved at a leisurely pace, keeping my eyes trained on the guy as he whipped a fly rod back and forth, then cast it far out in front of him. I peeked into his airboat as I passed by. There was nothing unusual or suspicious, just a few bags, tackle, and an extra rod.

I moved to within ten feet of him, then stopped. He didn't even turn around, just glanced over his shoulder.

"Thanks for scaring away all the fish," he said. He pulled in his line a few times, coiling it beside him, then added, "Something I can help you with?"

"Are you TJ Suggs?" I said.

He turned his head forward. "That depends on who's asking."

"I'll take that as a yes," I said. "You stayed at the Oyster Bay Chickee last night, right?"

He paused a moment, then shook his head.

"I don't know what you're talking about," he said, irritated.

"Relax," I said. "We're not the police. This is off the record."

"Oh—well, then, if you're not the police, I really don't know what you're talking about." He finished bringing in his line, then lifted his rod and whipped it back and forth a few times before tossing it perfectly, the light fly landing just a few feet shy of a tangle of mangrove branches. As he began to pull in slowly, he added, "Look, I come out here to get away from people. I'm a loner kind of guy. The last thing I want is to get caught up in some investigation."

"I can understand that," I said. "But those people you saw the other night, the ones that were murdered, they were friends of mine. They were good people. I look after my friends. I do whatever I can to help them. Just the way I'm wired."

He nodded, then paused a moment.

"Didn't know they were killed," he sighed and looked out over the water. He inhaled from his cigarette, burning it to the filter, then flicked it into the water. "I can respect that."

He pulled softly on the line, adjusting the fly's position and creating a small ripple, then turned and made eye contact with me for the first time since I'd approached him. He looked me over, pushed the curly hair out of his face as a gust of wind blew against us.

"I don't know much." He shrugged. "I was tired and hazy. Saw the first boat about an hour after sunset. Nice little skiff. Looked like a Carolina center-console with a good-sized outboard. Maybe around a hundred horsepower judging by its speed. The airboat cruised by less than a minute later. Both boats disappeared out across the bay. Heard gunshots soon after, then saw the smoke in the morning."

"Did you see how many guys were in the airboat?"

"There were two, I think. But it was dark and it was far off. Probably wouldn't have even noticed anything if I hadn't been taking a leak. The airboat looked old, but its engine ran well. Was closing in fast on the other boat. It didn't have any running lights or reflectors far as I could see."

"What were their headings?"

"Both swept into view out of Cormorant Pass, heading west. Then they cut south slightly toward Little Shark River."

I nodded. "And you saw nothing noteworthy about the guys? No physical characteristics at all?"

He shook his head and bit his lip.

"It all happened so fast. The guy in the pilot's seat looked big, though. Hard to tell for sure, but his head looked bald. All I saw was his silhouette, so take that with a shaker of salt." He grabbed a can of tobacco from his pocket, grabbed a pinch, and slid it into his left cheek. He spat a trail of juice and added, "I'll be back at the Flamingo this afternoon to restock up on supplies. We can talk some more then if you want."

I thanked him, then turned around. My mind was working overtime, trying to figure out what our next course of action should be. Most of the incidents seemed to point at a location near the mouth of the Watson River, so it was clear that we needed to start our search there.

Looking up, I saw Jack and Ange standing side

by side on the starboard pontoon of the Cessna just a few hundred feet away from me. I took two steps through the waist-deep water and the thick muddy bottom before a strong gust of wind blew into me. As I shielded my face from the wind, I heard a distinct foreign sound resonate from the east about a hundred feet off. It happened in an instant. A snapping sound, followed by the whoosh of an object as it rocketed past me just a few feet from my body. I spun my head around, nearly losing my balance, and watched with wide eyes as an arrow struck TJ in the back.

The sharp projectile tore into his body with such force that he keeled over and splashed into the water. I gasped, then narrowed my gaze and turned to look to the east, in the direction the arrow had flown from. I wanted to help TJ, to run over and provide assistance as quickly as possible. But whoever had loosed that arrow probably had more than one. If I didn't engage, there was a good chance I'd also end up facedown in the muck with an arrow sticking out of my back.

As fast as it could, my mind traced the trajectory of the arrow across the channel to a row of thick mangroves roughly two hundred feet away. The sudden surge of wind was still blowing steadily, causing branches to sway. I zeroed in, heard a branch snap, and caught a brief glimpse of a shadowy figure through cracks in the brush.

"Logan!" Ange yelled moments after TJ went down.

I kept my eyes locked, focused on the spot where I'd seen the attacker. In my blurry peripherals, I saw Ange and Jack still standing on the port pontoon. They were moving, no doubt taking cover or reaching for weapons.

"Help him!" I yelled.

Before the words left my mouth, I bolted in the direction of the attacker, splashing with reckless abandon into the murky channel. My heart pounded in my chest as I forced my body to slosh through the water and muddy bottom as fast as I could. If either Ange or Jack made any reply, I didn't hear it. I had tunnel vision and couldn't hear anything over the splashing water. The long stretch of mangrove-covered shoreline looked the same in both directions, and I knew that if I took my eyes off my target for even a moment, I'd lose my quarry.

As I bolted into the channel, the water quickly rose up past my waist. I reached the point where I could swim faster than I could run and dove headlong into the water. I utilized the combat sidestroke so that I could keep my head above water and my eyes trained forward.

With my clothes soaked and my senses fully alert, I reached the other side and climbed up out of the water. I looked ahead to where I'd seen movement while my right hand reached down and snatched my Sig from its holster under the right side of my waistband. The foliage was impossibly thick. A mangrove forest can be one of the hardest things in the world to navigate through, and every step was a struggle.

I heard Jack yell something from behind but couldn't process it. I heard only the rustling of leaves in the wind, the snapping of branches beneath me, and the distant movement up ahead of me. I was still a good distance away, and I knew that at any moment I could be struck by an arrow, so I kept my Sig raised as best I could just in case.

Regardless of the terrain or the slim chance of

my gaining ground, I pressed through with everything I had. There was a good chance that I was within a few hundred feet of the guy responsible for the Shepherds' murder, a guy who'd murdered a handful of people over the years. I wasn't about to pass up the opportunity to take him down, regardless of the risk.

The Florida summer sun beamed relentlessly into my face, causing sweat to drip down my face as I forced my way into what looked like a clearing up ahead. I could see water and a flat expanse of sawgrass through the breaks in the foliage. When I reached the opening, I spotted an airboat resting on the shoreline less than fifty feet away. Right in front of the boat stood a big guy with flabby tanned skin and a bald head. He wore a cutoff camo tee shirt, dirty baggy camo pants, and dirty boots that extended nearly up to his knees. His face was covered in mud and his eyes were concealed behind dark sunglasses.

He held a compound bow in his hands, the string drawn back, an arrow aimed straight at me. I didn't have time to take aim with my Sig. I could only dive to my left as he let go of the string, causing the limbs to snap and sending the arrow soaring less than a foot over my head. I rolled twice and steadied myself behind the thick trunk of a fallen cypress tree.

I was caught off guard by how fast he moved for such a big guy. Just a few seconds after the arrow zipped past, I peeked over the log just in time to see him jump into view and barrel straight into me. He tackled me hard, knocking the air from my lungs and sending us both crashing into a tangle of thick branches. I learned the painful way that not only was this guy fast, but he was also much heavier than I'd thought. His frame had to tip the scale at over three hundred pounds, and it felt like being tackled by a sumo wrestler as our weight cracked branches, my back oozing down into the mud below.

He grunted, exhaling a breath of disgusting air into my face. He held my gun down with his left hand and tried to stab a knife into my chest with his right. I held him back, gritting my teeth as his incredible strength inched the tip of the blade closer and closer. I gazed into his burning dark eyes and realized that this guy was enjoying having me pinned down.

Not for long, asshole.

In a flash of movement, I brought my head back, then snapped it forward, slamming my forehead hard into his nose. The fragile bones snapped like twigs, and blood rushed out from his nostrils as he groaned and jerked backward. With a few feet of space between us, I was able to bring up my right leg and kick my heel hard into his flabby belly. His upper body lurched forward, and he looked like he was about to barf as he let go of his knife.

As fast as I could, I rotated to the right, then scissor-kicked my legs, catching his ankles from both sides and causing his upper body to fall back. He fell hard against the cypress trunk and tumbled into the mud on the other side. I jumped to my feet and was about to stride over and finish him off when I suddenly realized that this wasn't a one-on-one fight.

A second guy was standing over by the airboat. He was almost as big as the first guy and was dressed similar aside from a skull bandanna that covered most of his face. He reached over the gunwale and grabbed a shiny silver object from inside. It took my mind a fraction of a second to process that it was a revolver. As he spun to face me, I reached back and slid my dive knife free from its sheath. Rearing it back, I took aim and sent it flying toward the guy just as the barrel of his weapon stared me down.

I aimed for the center of his chest but missed left. The blade struck him in the shoulder, causing his body to twist sideways. He grunted and loosened his grip on the revolver enough that it slid free and splashed into the shallow water at his feet.

I forced myself up and spun around just in time to see the first guy swing a tree branch straight at me. Before I could raise my hands or try and avoid the blow, the wood slammed into my head, nearly knocking me unconscious and sending me to the ground in a haze. My head screamed in pain and my vision blurred. I looked around, searching for a weapon, thinking that the big guy was moments away from closing in to finish me off. But he didn't. I watched with blurry eyes as he bolted for the airboat and helped the other guy to his feet.

I rolled over and forced myself up onto my hands and knees. My forehead burned and radiated sharp pain. I forced myself to breathe and tilted my head up toward my enemies. It took just a few blinks of my eyes for them to start up their airboat's massive engine, spin the propeller to life, and blow a strong gust of wind straight into me.

Through a haze, I saw that one of the guys was seated in the raised control chair, while the other stood alongside the port gunwale and aimed the silver revolver in my direction. I lowered my head and heard the explosion of a fired round, followed by the shattering of wood as it tore through the log.

I rolled over and looked around. After a few seconds, I spotted my Sig. It was upside down and lodged against the mud and a thick mangrove root. I kept low and crawled toward it. Reaching ahead of me as far as I could, I gripped the 9mm handgun, spun around, and took aim as I rose to my feet. The airboat was jetting across the water, its engine roaring, propelling it full speed away from me. It was already over a hundred yards away, but that wouldn't stop me from sending them a parting gift.

I lined up the sights and pulled the trigger in rapid succession, sending round after round into the back of the airboat and the fan cage. The two guys hit the deck, dropping out of view. By the time I let off the fifth round, they turned sharply, vanishing into a narrow channel and around a sharp corner of foliage. I could only hear them as the sounds of their fan and engine echoed across the water, growing fainter and fainter.

I lowered my weapon and caught my breath. My heart was still pounding violently, my adrenaline still surging. I couldn't believe we'd managed to find the killer so quickly. *Killers*, I corrected myself. We'd run into the killers and somehow I'd let them slip through my fingers.

I wished for a boat so that I could chase them down, but I knew that they were gone. I needed to shake the thoughts of them. I needed to get back to the others. If TJ was still alive, he'd need serious medical care, and fast.

I took in a deep breath, let it out, then spun around to face the imposing wall of mangroves I'd struggled through moments earlier. As I took my first step, I noticed a shiny blade glistening in the mud beside a patch of sawgrass. It wasn't my dive knife. No, my trusty titanium blade had been lodged in a serial killer's shoulder and was probably long gone by this point. It was one of their knives.

Before jumping back into the thick foliage, I grabbed the knife by the point, wrapped it in my small drybag, and stowed it carefully in my cargo shorts pocket. I had an idea that could help us figure out who these guys were. Maybe put a face and a name on at least one of the mysterious serial killers.

Holstering my Sig, I moved into the thick of it, heading back across the narrow island.

SEVEN

Jeb sat on the bow, his hand pressed against his bleeding shoulder. He groaned and grunted with every jerk of their airboat as Buck quickly brought them up to speed.

Suddenly, loud bangs rang out from behind them as a succession of bullets struck the transom and fan cage, shooting up sparks.

"Get down!" Buck shouted as he lowered himself while maintaining control of the speeding boat as best he could.

He cruised into a channel, then cut a hard left, putting a string of islands between them and their attacker. Looking over his shoulder, Buck could no longer see the mystery guy who'd chased him down. Regardless, he kept the throttles full as they cruised back into the northern section of Whitewater Bay.

"What the shit was that, Buck?" Jeb shouted. He slid down the bandanna covering the bottom half of his scarred face and added, "Who the hell was that asshole?"

Buck didn't reply. He kept his eyes narrowed, focused on the swamp ahead of him. He didn't know who the mystery guy with the plane was, but he was sure as hell going to find out.

Ten minutes after the confrontation, he eased back on the throttles, bringing them down to their cruising speed of twenty-five knots. They were five miles from where the fight had taken place. Since hightailing it out of there, they'd both kept sharp eyes out on the water around them and the sky above. Not having seen anything suspicious, Buck felt that they'd made it out of the woods. At least for the time being.

Buck sighed and grunted as he looked back over his shoulder for the hundredth time in the past few minutes alone.

It was supposed to be quick and easy, he thought.

Through a contact of theirs, they'd learned that Suggs had been the witness on Oyster Bay Chickee.

Take him out and put an end to the whole thing. But no. Some asshole flew in and disrupted our plans.

He gritted his teeth as he adjusted his shoulder. His body ached all over from the tussle. He knew that the guy he'd encountered wasn't an ordinary run-of-the-mill guy. And he sure as hell wasn't a cop. He'd barged right toward them with reckless abandon. A real trained warrior with no fear.

He maneuvered them around a large island, putting them on a northeasterly course.

Buck shook his head and glanced up at the sky. Something told him that their newfound enemy wasn't about to back down. That he'd come after them again, and keep coming after them until he'd either been killed or taken them out.

We need to take care of this guy, and we need to do it now.

"Get Eli on the radio, Jeb," Buck barked to the guy in the bow.

The bleeding guy lurched to the center of the boat and grabbed the radio out of a backpack. They had a basic first aid kit aboard, and he'd managed to stop the bleeding.

"Tell him to figure out who the guys were with the seaplane," he said.

Jeb did as he was told. He asked their informant for the intel, then placed the radio back in the backpack. Half an hour later, they reached their secret hideout far up into the bowels of the deep swamp. Later that evening, Eli called them on the radio.

"His name is Logan Dodge," he said through the crackling static. "I called around, and apparently he was once a Navy SEAL. I was told that he lives in Key West and keeps his boat at the Conch Harbor Marina. Man's garnered quite a reputation in the islands. He found the—"

"I don't need his whole damn life story," Buck snapped. "How many people does he have with him?"

Eli paused a moment.

"Three, I think. But this guy's got a lot of connections, it seems. Even knows Mitch Ross."

Buck lowered the radio and looked out over the endless uncharted swampland surrounding his hidden oasis. He placed his left thumb and index finger up to the bridge of his nose and squeezed. He knew that this guy was going to be a big pain in their ass. They needed to finish him off quickly and without question.

"You still there, Buck?" Eli said.

"I need you to kill them," Buck said by way of a reply. "I need them dead and gone. We'll pay you well for it, as usual."

"Did you hear what I said?" Eli retorted. "This guy's former special forces. How in the hell am I—"

"I'll send Jeb to help you out," Buck interrupted. "You're gonna have to play dirty. Engage in an unfair fight. Catch them by surprise. Whatever the hell you gotta do, you do it. Understand?"

Eli sighed.

"Buck, I—"

"Do you understand? Because this could mean the end of everything if we don't take this guy out!"

"Alright, alright," Eli said. "Yes, I understand. He's as good as dead. All of them are as good as dead."

Buck nodded.

"That's better. Jeb will meet you at midnight."

He turned off the radio before Eli could say any more. Lowering it to his side, he strode to the edge of a small bank above a murky shoreline. He slid off his backpack, pulled a piece of hog meat from a plastic bag, and tossed it into the water. Moments later, two gators splashed into the water and fought over the meat. He smiled as he watched the brutal predators go at it, then turned around when he heard footsteps approaching.

Jeb strode up to him. He was just as big as the other two guys and had burn scars covering much of his face from a childhood accident.

"When do I go?" Jeb said.

"Midnight," Buck replied. "You will meet with Eli, and the two of you will kill them."

Jeb smiled and nodded.

"Lookin' forward to it."

EIGHT

I reached the other side of the narrow island just as Ange and Jack were lifting TJ's limp body up into the Cessna. Stepping out onto a thick branch, I dove headfirst into the murky water and swam as fast as I could to the other side. I reached the port pontoon of the plane just as Ange started up the engine. Jack held on to the wing brace and leaned over, offering his right hand to help pull me up out of the water. I was soaked and exhausted, and my head still hurt like hell from being struck with a log.

"Nice to see you don't have any arrows sticking out of you," Jack said. "You alright?"

I nodded. Ange glanced over her shoulder and looked me up and down with a worried gaze. I mouthed that I was alright, and she turned her attention back to the plane's controls. It was clear from her expression that we didn't have time to sit around and talk about what had just happened. We needed to get in the air and we needed to find a doctor, fast.

Her gaze darted down to the anchor line.

"Give me a hand," I said, tapping Jack on the shoulder.

We quickly pulled the anchor up, coiled the line, and stowed it in the pontoon's rear compartment. Seconds later we were climbing inside, Jack sliding into the back seat beside TJ and me in the copilot's seat. Ange had us accelerating forward just as we sat, bringing us into a small bay with plenty of room to take off.

As she brought us up to speed, I turned around and looked back at TJ. He was resting on his side against the padded gray seat, his body angled slightly. Blood soaked his thin flannel shirt and the top of his pants. His eyes were closed and he was struggling for every breath.

Jack had a first aid kit open on his lap and was tearing into a packet of QuikClot. He pressed a few pads around the wound, right where the arrow was still sticking out. If the arrow had broadheads like the ones we'd found stuck in the dinghy earlier that morning, pulling it free would cause further damage and bleeding.

I helped Jack slow the bleeding as Ange pulled back, lifting us up off the water. The bouncing over the slightly white-capped bay gave way to a smooth upward ride.

"I need a course, guys!" Ange shouted.

Neither Jack nor I had donned headsets, so it was the only way to hear her over the roar of the engine.

"Closest should be the Mariners Hospital in Tavernier," Jack yelled back.

He reached beside his seat and grabbed the cardboard tube containing the Everglades charts as well as a map of southern Florida. Since we didn't have a signal for the GPS, we'd have to rely on them to find a good landing site.

I spun around, pulled out the map, and did a quick measurement before donning my headset.

"Roughly twenty-eight miles southeast of us, Ange," I said.

She nodded and turned us around, putting us on a direct course for the Upper Keys. I looked closely at the map, looking for a good place for us to drop down.

"Near Point Lowe looks like our best bet," I said, pointing at a place on the map while holding it in front of Ange. "There's a public ramp here. It's on the Atlantic side, and this wind will make it choppy, but it's nothing you can't handle."

She nodded confidently.

Once I had a signal on my smartphone, I looked up the number to the hospital. When I had a woman from dispatch on the line, I explained the situation and requested an ambulance to meet us at the boat ramp at the eastern end of Lowe Street.

Ange brought us down a few minutes later, landing just past the outstretched planks of a few private docks. As expected, the water was choppy and we bounced a few times before slowing to just a few knots. Ange motored us into a small man-made marina just as an ambulance pulled up alongside an old dock. Even over the engine, we could hear its siren screaming across the morning air.

I opened the starboard door as we motored up alongside the dock, tied us off, and helped a team of first responders put TJ onto a stretcher and carry him off the plane. Quickly and efficiently, the professionals loaded him into the back of the ambulance. We watched as the siren switched on again and they swiftly disappeared down Lowe Street, heading toward the center of the island.

My heart was still pounding as the sound died away. It didn't look good for him. I'd seen a lot of mortal injuries before, and getting struck by an arrow to the back was right up there. A blow like that could routinely take down a full-grown six-hundred-pound elk if placed correctly. I was amazed he'd survived the flight.

"Shit, bro," Jack said as he looked over at me. The three of us were standing at the end of the dock, right beside the tied-off Cessna. He motioned up toward the sky and added, "Not even noon yet and we're already in the thick of it."

Jack was right. It was hard to believe we'd taken off from Tarpon Cove Marina earlier that very morning.

"What happened with you anyway?" Ange said, wrapping an arm around me and looking at me with her beautiful blue eyes. "If it'd been anyone else, I'd have been worried." She brushed a few hairs from my face, her fingers sliding over the side of my head. "Crap, Logan. You're bleeding."

Her eyes grew wide as she touched a cut. It stung a little. She stepped beside me, reached into the backseat, and pulled out a packet of antiseptic wipes and a large Band-Aid.

"I'm fine," I said. "Little dizzy. The guy used my head for batting practice and made pretty solid contact."

"I'll say," Ange said, wiping the wound and making it sting even more.

"You get a good look at him, bro?"

I shook my head.

"They were both wearing face paint and

79

sunglasses."

They paused, looked at each other, then looked back at me.

"Both?" Ange said.

"Yeah. Looks like we've got two crazy serial killers on our hands. Just our luck."

"I'll make sure and buy a few lottery tickets," Ange said. "So what now?"

"I got a message from Pete," Jack said. "He made it to Flamingo."

I nodded. "We'll head over there in a bit and meet him. Just need to stop by the post office first."

I reached into my cargo shorts pocket and pulled out the killer's knife, which was still wrapped up in my drybag. I'd done my best to preserve it and hoped that the fingerprints hadn't worn off. After a quick taxi ride, I mailed the knife same-day air to my old friend Scott Cooper. Scott had been my division officer in the Navy, and we'd been good friends ever since. Smart, athletic, and good at just about everything, Scott was currently serving as a senator representing Florida. He had a lot of connections, and I knew that he'd be able to get the knife into the right hands.

After mailing it off, we rode back to the dock. I called Mitch from the backseat and gave him a quick rundown of what'd happened. I also told him that TJ's airboat was tied off just south of Hells Bay Chickee and that somebody would need to pick it up.

Just as the sun reached the top of the sky, we boarded the Cessna and flew northeast, back across Florida Bay.

NINE

We soared at a cruising speed of a hundred and fifty knots. Just under ten minutes after taking off, Ange brought us down a few hundred yards off Flamingo Beach. She motored us past the large pink Everglades National Park Headquarters and ranger station buildings and brought us into Flamingo Marina. We pulled up to a dock across from the Baia, and Ange killed the engine.

Aside from the Baia, a small dinghy, and a pontoon boat, the ocean side of the marina was empty, leaving a large selection of vacant spots along the various docks. Made sense. The Everglades isn't exactly a popular tourist destination in the summer months. From June through September, the Glades boast average highs above ninety degrees with enough humidity to soak a sponge. And then there are the bugs. During a python-hunting trip, Jack had once told me that major companies and the US military use the Everglades to test bug sprays to see if they work at repelling mosquitoes. All in all, the summer Glades experience usually results in even the most prepared visitors adjusting their vacation plans at the last minute.

I removed my headset, stowed it on the dash, and pushed open the door. A rush of hot air swept against me. The moment my feet hit the starboard pontoon, I heard a familiar barking sound. As I bent down to tie us off, Atticus jumped the small gap onto the dock and buried his face in my chest. I smiled broadly and wrapped an arm around him while looping the nylon rope around the cleats.

Ange and Jack climbed down and we hauled our gear out of the cockpit and pontoon storage compartments. Pete appeared on the Baia's deck and stepped onto the dock, offering us a hand. I thanked him for coming and for bringing up my boat.

"Don't mention it," he said, waving a hand at me. "Mitch told me you made some friends over in Hells Bay."

"You could say that," I said, loading our bags onto the Baia and carrying them down into the salon.

When we returned topside, Pete opened my cooler and handed out a few ice-cold bottles of water. I twisted one open and chugged all of it down in one long pull. I'd been so focused that I hadn't realized how thirsty I was, and the water felt amazing.

"We need to talk about what happened," Ange said.

I nodded. "Yeah, we do." We'd only been able to discuss the incident briefly during the taxi rides and the flight back. "Just give me a minute. I'm in desperate need of a shower."

"Yeah, you are," Pete joked. "I was about to say that you should get your money back for whatever deodorant spray you're using."

We laughed as I turned, stepped below deck, and headed straight for the main cabin. I stripped off my clothes, which had undergone a lap in murky swamp water, treks through mangroves, and a few hours under the hot sun, and tossed them into a small hamper. After a quick hot shower, I dressed in a fresh tee shirt, shorts, and sandals.

Everyone was gathered in the salon when I stepped out. They had a big chart of the southern Everglades spread out on the dinette and were in the middle of a conversation.

"And that's when this guy Teagan Suggs was struck in the back by an arrow," Jack said just as I appeared.

"Then Logan went for a swim," Ange said.

I nodded as I hinged open my fridge. "Seemed like a good way to cool off."

I realized right away that Pete had taken the liberty of fully stocking my galley for the trip. There was a stack of fish fillets folded in pages of the *Keynoter*, a row of coconut water, four six-packs of Paradise Sunset beers, and a plastic bag of various fruit.

"I figured you'd be needing some good food if you were gonna go after a serial killer," Pete said. "Speaking of good food, the Flamingo food truck just rolled in an hour ago. Let's take this conversation to dry land. I want to hear what happened after your little swim."

The food truck was parked in the lot beside the marina office. After paying the moorage fees for the Cessna, we ordered a stack of Cuban sandwiches along with potato chips and lemonades. We carried our haul over to a picnic table on the grass beside the water, which was well shaded thanks to a row of lignum vitae trees.

As we ate the sandwiches, which were much better than I'd expected, I told them what had happened starting from the moment I'd confronted the two guys near Hells Bay. Unfortunately, there wasn't much to tell. I knew their body types, how they were dressed, and their choice of weapons, but little else.

Once I'd told them what had happened, Pete steered the conversation to our search at the wreck.

"You guys find anything there?" he asked.

Ange rose and moved toward the water, down the dock, and into her Cessna. She returned less than a minute later with one of the arrows we'd pulled from the dinghy.

"We found this," she said, presenting it to Pete.

Pete grabbed it and examined it for a few seconds. "Carbon shaft. Broadhead tip. Decent weight, I'd say five hundred grain. Scratched off all manufacturer markings."

"Right." Jack nodded. "And it's a match to the one used to shoot the guy in Hells Bay."

Pete nodded, taking everything in. "Find anything else?"

The three of us exchanged glances.

"Yeah," I said. "We may have found a motive."

He'd been looking out over the water, but his eyes suddenly darted over to meet mine.

"A motive?" he said.

"Ange found a bag of coke in their dink," Jack said. "I didn't know the Shepherds all that well, but something tells me that it wasn't with them when they motored into the Glades."

"Cocaine?" Pete said, shaking his head. "There's no way George would have that kind of contraband.

84

He was as law-abiding as a citizen can get, straighter than this arrow." Pete paused a moment, taking a drink of his lemonade. "So the Shepherds stumbled upon a bag of snow, then these killers chase after them for it. These killers must be drug dealers." He looked around the group and we each nodded. That was the conclusion we'd reached as well. "Who have you told about the coke?"

"Nobody," I said. "And we'd like to keep it close to the chest until we can figure more of this out."

We talked for half an hour while finishing up our food. I kept Atticus entertained by tossing his tennis ball across the grass a few times. I was surprised when he wore himself out after just a handful of throws. I guess he was enjoying the heat and humidity about as much as we were. I'd just showered and changed, yet my clothes were already starting to feel sticky.

As we gathered up our trash, I noticed a boat pull up on the freshwater side of the marina. After a quick tie-off, a tall guy with tanned skin and a long black beard stormed straight across the parking lot toward where the Baia and Cessna were floating. He was dressed in full camouflage and wore muddy hip boots. He paused for a moment along the water, staring at the dock, then turned and thundered toward us. It didn't take me long to realize that he was the same guy we'd seen earlier, the one who'd shaken a fist at us as we'd flown over him while looking for TJ in Hells Bay.

"This one of your brawling buddies, Logan?" Pete said, rising to his feet and hovering his right hand over his waistband.

I didn't need to see under his shirt to know that his silver Taurus Raging Bull revolver was stowed there, ready to be withdrawn and utilized at a moment's notice.

"No," Ange said, answering for me. "We saw him from the air. Didn't look happy to see us then either."

I stepped in front of the group and stood tall, facing the oncoming stranger. Whoever he was and whatever he wanted, he was trying to intimidate us with his movements. It didn't work. I had my Sig ready at the side of my waistband just in case, but I was confident I could handle this guy unarmed.

"Well, if it isn't the city boy who scared off my kill," he said.

He was wearing a ball cap and sunglasses, but it was clear from his body language and tone that he was pissed off. He stepped right up to me, moving his face less than a foot away from mine. I pegged him as a typical wannabe tough guy who lacked discernment when picking a fight. All brawn, no brains.

"You don't want any trouble," I said, staring at him through his dirty sunglasses. My body stayed tall, not moving back even an inch. "But if you don't get out of my face, you're gonna have a lot of it."

He snarled and furrowed his brow. His left hand formed a fist and I could tell that he was close to making a decision that he was going to regret.

Just then, a second guy approached. This one came from behind me, and in my peripherals, I saw that he was wearing a round-brimmed tan hat, a short-sleeved gray button-up with a gold badge, and green pants. The angry guy in front of me shifted his gaze to the approaching guy, then took a small step backward.

"Am I too late to place a bet?" the guy said.

His tone was casual, but his voice was raised. He

walked over and stopped between me and Angry Guy. He was a few inches shorter than me, had lightly tan skin, and looked to be in his forties. His distinct Texan drawl and park ranger uniform made it obvious who he was.

"You must be Logan Dodge," he said, turning to look at me and extending his right hand. When I accepted it, he added, "I'm Mitch Ross. Nice to finally meet you in person." He glanced over at the other guy. "And I see you've met Hank Boggs. A frequent happy face around these parts. You giving these folks a good Gladers welcome, Hank?"

"These slickers scared off my quarry with their damn low-flying plane," Hank snarled. He was still breathing heavily. "I was just about to put it down. First hog I've seen in two days."

"I'm sure you'll find another," Mitch said. "I promise you that it wasn't the only one out there."

Hank stepped beside me and faced Mitch.

"You have any idea how long I was stalking that boar? It was all a waste of time thanks to these tourists here."

"Right," Ange said. "I'm sure your time is very valuable."

I cracked a smile. Even the brute caught her sarcasm.

"You wanna say that again, little girl?" he said, stepping toward her.

Ange didn't back down. She strode toward him confidently and I stepped between them at the last second. Hank had a rage-fueled look in his eyes that I was all too familiar with. Before either of them could make a move on the other, I grabbed Hank by his left wrist, twisted his body around, and slammed his head against the picnic table. It wasn't hard enough to knock him out, but it was hard enough to cause him to grunt and flare his nostrils.

I pressed him against the tabletop while forcing his arm behind him. In that position, I could break his arm in a fraction of a second if necessary.

"Time for you to cool off," I said sternly. "If you make a move like that again, I'll break you. Understand?"

He was still breathing heavily, but his muscles relaxed a little and he nodded. I let go of him and stepped back, letting him regain himself. He rubbed his forehead, then spat onto the grass.

"You're welcome," I said.

He rubbed his jaw and sneered.

"What the hell for?"

"For saving your ass," I said. "'Cause this 'little girl' was about to hand it to you."

He narrowed his gaze again, but this time Mitch stepped in.

"Easy, Hank," Mitch said. "They're here to help with the investigation." Mitch paused a moment, then added, "Come to think of it, you were out in the center of Whitewater the other night, right? You didn't see anything? Didn't hear any gunshots?"

Hank gathered himself. Took one last look at us, then turned around and stormed back toward his airboat.

"This is the Glades," he yelled as he walked away. "Gunshots go off all the time."

Mitch watched him for a few seconds, then turned to look at us.

Jack shook his head and chuckled. "We're just making all sorts of new friends today, aren't we?"

TEN

"I hope you don't judge the people in this neck of the woods by your interactions today," Mitch said as he led us over to the ranger station building. "I've lived all over the country and I've never met so many friendly people in my life. Barring a few exceptions, of course."

The cool air inside felt amazing, whooshing against us as we entered through the glass door. There was a small welcome area with a counter full of maps and pamphlets on the park. A few stuffed raccoon and a deer rested on shelves off to the side. I'd been there a few times before and spotted a familiar friendly face behind the counter.

"Hey, Martha," I said, waving toward her as we walked across the room. "It's good to see your bright and smiling face."

She walked around the counter and greeted all of us.

"This is a nice surprise after the tough couple of days we've had," she said with a smile. She looked at my face and added, "Logan, what kind of trouble have you gotten into this time?"

I feigned confusion, then grinned and told her that it was barely a scratch.

She moved back around the corner to her usual place in front of her computer screen. I recognized the donation jar with the black Wounded Warrior emblem beside her keyboard. She always encouraged the dropping of spare change into the tin, even if it was just a penny. There was also a new jar that I hadn't seen there before. It had a picture taped to it of a young woman holding onto her baby. It took me a few seconds, but I realized that it was Anne Cody.

"Thank you for this," I said, motioning toward the jar as we passed by.

She sighed and replied, "Anything I can do to help that poor woman."

Anne was the young widow of Ryan Cody, a Coast Guard rescue swimmer who'd been killed along with two other guardsmen last summer. Their helicopter had been blown to pieces by an RPG fired by a Cuban gang member on Loggerhead Key. I'd been on the island when it had happened. I'd watched the explosion, and Ryan had died in my arms.

I tried not to relive that memory as Mitch led us down a hallway, then up a set of stairs. His office was simple, just a desk with a laptop and rows of metal filing cabinets. There was a window on the opposite side that looked out toward the grassy waterfront beside the marina. I could see the picnic table we'd just been eating at and figured that was how Mitch had seen our little confrontation.

We gathered around the desk with Atticus at our feet. We unfolded a chart of the Everglades and gave Mitch a quick rundown of what had happened. When we finished, I asked him if he'd received an update on TJ.

"He passed away," Mitch said with a sigh. "Got off the phone with the hospital in Tavernier just a few minutes before I saw Hank walking up to pay you guys a visit."

We fell silent for a few seconds.

"I'm sorry to hear that," I said. "Though I was amazed he'd survived so long after receiving such a blow."

"It's also amazing that you managed to get so close to these killers and walk away from it," Mitch said. "Most people can't say that. You get him back for that?"

He motioned to my forehead, where the Band-Aid covered my cut.

"No, but I did bury my dive knife in his buddy's shoulder," I said. "Which reminds me, you guys don't happen to sell knives in that store of yours, do you?"

"There's a few fishing and hunting knives," Mitch replied.

I nodded, making a mental note to stop by and pick up a new blade.

"Have you had any reports today?" Ange said. "After the shooting near Hells Bay, did anyone see anything suspicious?"

Mitch nodded. "Got a call from a local. Said he saw an airboat hauling ass into Whitewater, heading northwest. Said it was just after hearing all the gunfire. He also said one of them looked injured."

"Northeast across Whitewater," Pete said, looking down at the chart. "Haven't most of the incidents occurred near the mouth of the Watson River?"

Mitch nodded. "There's a cluster around there.

Which could explain why these guys were motoring in that direction."

"Some kind of home base," Ange said.

"Maybe," Mitch said. "But that river and the entire area around its mouth has been searched dozens of times over the years. No sign of a shelter has ever been found."

"Well, they're out there somewhere," I said, looking down at the chart. "What about this Hank character? You know him well? Because he had a release sticking out of his pocket."

A release is a small metal pincher that straps around your wrist and is used to draw back an arrow, making it easier and taking the pressure off your fingers.

Mitch shook his head. "Don't know him too well. It's his first year down here, far as I know. He certainly has a hot temper. As far as the release goes, most boats in the Glades this time of year will have a bow. We're right at the beginning of archery season."

I leaned back, looked out his office window and stared at the Cessna tied off in the marina. Ange glanced over at me and read my mind.

"The longer we wait, the colder this trail gets," she said. "We need to get back out there."

"Where will you head?" Mitch asked.

I pointed at the mouth of the Watson River.

"Looks like the evidence points to here."

Before heading back into the heat, I bought a new hunting knife from their store to replace my lost dive knife. They didn't have a big selection, but I ended up purchasing a beautiful knife with a six-inch steel blade and a polished cherrywood handle. Mitch told me that it was made by a local knifemaker up in Orlando and that their knives had a good reputation around the world.

Once I had my new knife sheathed and strapped to the back of my waistband, we stepped outside and hauled our gear from the Baia across to the freshwater side of the marina. Pete had taken the liberty of securing us the use of an airboat. With its flat-bottomed design and no operating parts below the waterline, airboats are the ideal mode of transportation in the marshy landscape of the Everglades.

"She used to be a tour boat," Pete said. "But the front row of seats was removed, so there's plenty of space for everyone and the gear. Plus this five-fifty-hp supercharged engine will push her through the water at over fifty knots."

We loaded everything up, topped off the fuel, and climbed aboard. It was just after 1400, so we still had five hours of daylight left to motor up into the Glades, take a look around, and set up camp for the night.

"How long you think you'll be out for?" Mitch asked.

"Probably just a few days," I lied.

The truth was, I wasn't coming back until the killers were gator food. I didn't care how long it took.

"Alright," he said. "I'll be just a call away if you need anything. And I'll keep you updated. You guys got a radio?"

"And a sat phone. It's the number I called you on earlier this morning."

He nodded and helped us untie the lines. "I just got off the phone with Eli Hutt. He's the local who spotted the airboat earlier. He said he'll be near the Watson River Chickee if you want to meet up with him."

We had a general location and we had an eyewitness. It wasn't a lot to go on, but it would have to work.

We were all aboard except Pete and Mitch, who were both right beside us on the dock.

"My friend from the Seminole tribe's driving down here early in the morning," Pete said. "I'm gonna stay here and meet him. We'll head over and catch up with you guys tomorrow. This guy can be a lot of help to us. His family has lived in this part of the state for hundreds of years." He paused a moment and added, "Just try not to get yourselves into too much trouble until we join you guys."

"Staying out of trouble isn't exactly my strong suit," I said. "Especially after two of my friends are murdered."

"I'll watch him closely, don't worry," Ange said, elbowing me softly.

"Here, bro," Jack said, handing me a set of earmuffs and earplugs. "We're gonna want double hearing protection for this beast."

We all donned the earplugs and muffs, including Atticus. Mitch had brought over a special pair from the marina office that strapped around his head to stay in place. It bothered him at first, but he was a smart dog and seemed to catch on quick.

We sat on the bench seat and Atticus stood at the bow while Jack fired up the engine. The massive eighty-two-inch-diameter five-blade propeller spun to life. It cast a whirlwind over the water behind us. As Jack motored us away from the dock and into the channel, we turned around and gave them a quick wave. When I directed my gaze forward, I focused on the world in front of me and did my best to prepare for what I knew was going to be a long evening.

ELEVEN

Jack accelerated us past a large alligator that was sunbathing on a muddy shoreline, then turned us north into Buttonwood Canal, a three-mile-long, fifty-foot-wide channel that stretches from the Flamingo Marina up into Coot Bay. He kept us slow enough through the canal so that we could spot manatees in our path. The large marine mammals also known as sea cows have become endangered, and many of their deaths can be attributed to reckless, oblivious boaters.

When we entered and began crossing Coot Bay, we passed by an airboat pulling a second one in tow. The pilot wore the same tan park ranger uniform that Mitch had been wearing and shot us a wave before continuing on the way we'd just come. I'd seen the airboat in tow before. It was TJ's boat. One of the other rangers had motored out into Hells Bay, tied it off, and was taking it back to Flamingo.

I've seen more than my share of death and have witnessed the repercussions of evil firsthand many times. It's never gotten easier for me to wrap my head around. I didn't know Teagan Suggs, but I did know that he had a mom and a dad. Hell, he'd probably been married with kids. Probably had a handful of loved ones who cared about him. And now he was gone. His life had been taken in a swift act of brutal hostility by a murdering psychopath.

I thought about the others who'd died here over the years, especially the Shepherds. Thought about how their families must have reacted when they'd gotten the news. It wasn't a pleasant thought, but it was real, and it was powerful. It struck a chord deep within me, strengthening my resolve even more.

Jack navigated us into Whitewater Bay, the massive inlet of the Gulf of Mexico. The wind had died off a little from earlier that morning but was still blowing strong enough to make it clear how the bay had gotten its name. We weaved through a seemingly never-ending landscape of water and thick green islands and reached the Watson River Chickee ten miles across the bay.

Ange and I kept our eyes peeled and our heads on a swivel. Every time we passed a boat, we'd grab the binoculars and take a look. As I'd expected, we saw no sign of the two big guys from earlier that morning. After years of killing and getting away with it, these guys had a strong system in place for keeping themselves hidden.

When we arrived at the Watson River Chickee, we spotted three tents already set up and four kayaks tied off to the leeward side. They were all those long, skinny expensive-type lightweight kayaks that offer minimum drag and maximum efficiency in the water. Whitewater Bay is ten miles long and six miles wide. It consists of mostly shallow waters that are easily manipulated by even subtle changes in tide, current, and wind. Kayaking here isn't for beginners.

We pulled up to the chickee from the south. It was situated at the tip of an island, so we weren't able to see the whole thing until we motored in front of it. Once we were close, we saw two guys sitting Indian style on the edge of the planks. They were both lean guys, with long hair, bandannas, and sport sunglasses. When Jack killed the big engine, two women stepped out from one of the tents. Both were lean young women with no tan lines. They were each wearing a pair of panties and nothing else.

"Good evening," I said, removing my ear protection and stepping to the starboard bow, putting on my friendliest face.

Atticus jumped over beside me and wagged his tail as he looked over at the new faces.

The two guys were closest to us, so I addressed them. I'd expected the young women to get embarrassed by their appearance as our airboat floated right alongside the chickee, but they were unfazed. They stepped right over beside the two guys, their upper bodies on full display.

"Nice... boats," Jack said, his voice a little more awkward than usual.

The girls laughed.

"Thanks," one of them replied, shooting Jack a seductive look.

The two men paused a moment, then one of them nodded.

"They better be after how much we paid for them," he said. "Like most hobbies, it's as expensive as you want it to be."

I smiled and nodded.

"A boat is just a hole in the water to throw money into," I said. "At least these aren't very big

97

holes."

He laughed and shot me a friendly look back. We'd only exchanged a few brief words, but that was all it took. It's always the deal when you encounter someone you've never met before. It's a quick calculation you make. Self-preservation. *Is this person crazy?* you ask yourself. It's especially true when you meet someone in the middle of nowhere, far from the arm of the law.

Dreadlocks at least seemed somewhat normal, though he certainly had some excessively liberal female companions.

I glanced around the group and made eye contact with one of the girls. She was looking at me in a way that made me feel uncomfortable, especially when standing next to my wife.

"We're supposed to meet a few friends here," I said, looking back to Dreadlocks. "Any of you happen to see a couple of big guys in an airboat motor past a few hours ago?"

Dreadlocks shook his head. "Sorry. We just arrived half an hour ago. Haven't seen anyone."

"Yeah, we did, Ronnie," one of the women said. She looked slightly older than the other girl and had fiery red hair and about a dozen visible tattoos. "That guy who approached us earlier."

"Oh, right. He came alongside us in a little boat while we were paddling. Seemed like a nice guy. Said his name was Eli, I think. Tried to offer us some gator jerky, but we're on a strict diet."

"We're *vegans*," the red-haired woman said.

Ange chuckled at the way she said it, though she kept it quiet enough for only Jack and me to notice.

"And where'd you guys come in from?" I asked.

"We started at Highland Beach early this

morning. We saw him a few miles west of here. Doubt he was one of your friends, though. I bet he weighs less than I do, and I'm a buck sixty soaking wet. A dwarf wouldn't call that guy big."

"That's a long way to paddle in one day," Jack said.

"We're training to complete the Everglades challenge," the younger girl said. "It's a three-hundred-mile kayak race that begins all the way up near Tampa and finishes in Key Largo."

"I've heard of it," Jack said. "That's very impressive."

She shot another flirty smile at Jack.

The race sparked my interest, and I stowed the information away for another time.

"Thanks for your time," I said and nodded to Jack. "Let's get going."

If we couldn't meet up with Eli, I wanted to get our drone up in the air as soon as possible.

"You sure you can't stay?" the red-haired woman said. "We have plenty of space."

She motioned toward the planks beside her. Nearly every inch of the small platform was already covered by their tents.

"We already have accommodations," Ange said.

The two girls shot her a jealous look, and the red-haired one put her hands on her hips. I smiled and motioned to Jack, who was already climbing back into the control seat.

"Wish I could be of more help," Dreadlocks said with a shrug.

I thanked him anyway, and we donned our hearing protection. Jack started up the engine and roared us over to the mouth of the Watson River less than half a mile north of the chickee. Like almost everywhere in the Glades, the water was slow-moving and dark. I stepped up to the bow and took a look around while Jack tied us off to a small patch of mangroves. The coast was clear aside from the kayakers far in the distance at our back.

"Jack, I think your mouth's still open," Ange said with a laugh.

He shrugged. "No shame here. Those girls were knockouts."

After helping tie off the airboat, I moved toward the center.

"Come on," I said, grabbing a plastic hardcase from the deck. "Let's get this thing fired up."

Within minutes we had our new drone out, hooked up, and soaring up into the air. It was top-of-the-line, and though we'd only used it a few times, the controls were simple and smooth. It was a quadcopter, so it had four thrusters that allowed the craft to remain stable. We utilized all of its three-mile range, flying it upriver and recording footage of the ground using its high-definition camera. The camera also allowed us to see where we were going by syncing up wirelessly to my laptop.

It was like a never-ending maze, an intricate world of waterways, swamps, bogs, and grass. After twenty minutes of searching, we had nothing. No boats, people, or structures of any kind near the main section of the river. Not even a line of smoke from a burning fire.

"Looks like we're about to have company," Jack said just after we landed the drone.

Ange and I were examining the small flying machine, making sure everything was working correctly, while Jack stood beside the control seat. He was facing southeast and staring through a pair of

100

binoculars. Atticus, who'd been lounging in the shade under the bench seat, shuffled out from his spot and looked off in the same direction as Jack.

Listening, I could hear the low hum of an engine growing louder and louder. An airboat appeared soon after. The hull was old and beat to hell, but the engine looked and sounded decent. A short skinny guy pulled up beside us and killed his engine, his boat drifting to within ten feet of ours.

He smiled broadly as he removed his earmuffs, stepped over to his starboard bow, and gave us a friendly wave. He looked around fifty years old, with leathery skin and a wiry build. He wore jeans and a Harley Davidson tee shirt that looked a few sizes too big for him.

"Name's Eli," he said in a deep Southern accent. "What brings y'all to the area? You don't look like hunters."

But we are hunters, I thought. *We aren't after boar, deer, or gator, however. We're after the most dangerous of all big game.*

"Eli Hutt?" I said.

He raised his eyebrows and tilted his sunglasses down to get a better look. The sun was barely hanging on and was casting bright rays over the bay.

"I'm sorry, I don't believe I've ever met y'all before."

"You haven't," I said. "But we have a mutual friend. Mitch Ross. He told us what you saw earlier today."

His eyes widened, his mouth dropped open a little, and he nodded.

"Ah, right. You must be Logan."

I nodded, then introduced Ange and Jack.

"Pleasure to meet y'all," he said. Then he leaned

101

forward and lowered his voice, as if there could be someone listening in the middle of nowhere. "Any luck tracking down the guys from this morning?"

If we'd had any luck, they'd both be making their way through a gator's digestion system at that very moment.

"No," I said. "Seen anything else?"

"Not since this morning."

"Which way did they go?" Ange asked. "They head upriver?"

Eli shrugged. "Couldn't tell ya. I only saw them over near Midway Pass. They were headed in this direction, that's all I know."

"Mitch says you've spent a lot of time in the Glades over the years," I said. "You seem pretty nonchalant about all this. The close proximity of these killers doesn't bother you?"

Eli shook his head and smiled, revealing a few gold teeth.

"He doesn't scare me none," he said.

He reached into the back of his waistband and pulled out a tarnished steel-colored revolver with a smooth walnut grip. It was a handgun I'd recognize a mile away, a Colt M1917 .45.

My right hand hovered over my Sig.

"I keep my Colt within arm's reach at all times," he added. "I fought in 'Nam. Had it since then. Anyone tries to pull something on me and they're gonna get filled with lead, simple as that."

I was slightly irritated but did my best not to show it. When Mitch had mentioned Eli back at Flamingo, he'd made it sound like the guy could help us. Now it turned out that he knew less than we did.

"Getting kinda late," he said, looking up at the sky. "All the chickees nearby are filled up. Y'all have

102

a place to set up camp for the night?"

Before Jack or Ange could answer, I said, "Yeah."

And that was all I said. It was a lie, of course. But I didn't feel like delving into the truth.

Eli raised his hands into the air.

"Didn't mean to pry, friend," he said. "I've got a place inland just down the way. It's a secret camp in the middle of that island there." He pointed to a small mangrove-infested island roughly half a mile southwest of us. "There's plenty of room for y'all. You'd have to bring your own tents, though. Mine's a little small, and the bugs here will eat ya alive."

"I appreciate the offer," I said.

"And it's on the table all night. I'll have the fire going." He stepped back over to the control seat of his airboat and grabbed his earmuffs. "Y'all want some gator jerky?"

I waved him off.

"We've got plenty of food. Thanks for the offer, though."

He nodded, smiled broadly, and told us to have a good night before starting up the engine and roaring toward his secret island camp.

"Is it just me, or does that guy give off a strange vibe?" Jack said.

"It's not just you," Ange said. "I can't tell if he's Ned Flanders or Ted Bundy. What do you think, Logan?"

I kept my eyes trained out over the water, watching as his airboat motored away from us.

"I think we need to set watches for tonight," I said. "I don't want anyone creeping up on us while we sleep."

"Speaking of sleep," Jack said, "where exactly is

103

this camp of ours?"

I took a quick look around. Options were slim. We had the choice between alligator-infested murky water or patches of land with foliage so thick you couldn't even see the ground. Then my eyes gravitated to the large deck at our feet.

"With the seats removed, this boat looks big enough to set up our tents," I said.

Jack bent down and rapped the aluminum hull with his knuckles.

"Couldn't have thought up a harder surface to sleep on?" he said.

"It's not ideal," I said, "but sometimes in the pursuit of justice, you've got to deal with a little discomfort. It comes with the territory."

"Who said that?" Jack said, raising his eyebrows at me. "It sounds like something Batman would say."

We opened the cooler and pulled out the sandwiches Ange had made before leaving the house in Key West. After washing it all down with water, we sat around the maps and charts and planned out what we'd do the next day. It wasn't long before the sun started to fall. We set up our tents and sprayed about a gallon of bug spray each, knowing that the tiny pests would come swarming with the cooler air.

I've always enjoyed watching the sunset. I make an effort to watch the artistic glowing exit every evening, especially when I'm out on the water. But tonight was different. Tonight, all my thoughts were elsewhere and I kept my head down as we looked over maps and brainstormed what course of action to take next. I glanced up only a few times, just enough to catch part of the show and to feel the warmth on my face before everything faded into darkness.

Just before calling it a night at 2200, we came to

the conclusion that we were going to head upriver the following morning. I didn't care how long it took. I was resolved to search every single tributary if I had to in order to find these guys.

Ange took the first watch and I relieved her at midnight. Atticus seemed to really appreciate the cool of the evening. He'd stayed up with her and kept me company for half an hour before passing out beside me. It was dark and intensely quiet. I kept myself occupied by running over scenarios in my mind. When going after bad guys, you need to think like they do, but putting myself into the frame of mind of a sadistic serial killer proved difficult. I thought about my fight with them that morning. I thought about the cocaine Ange had found. And I thought about the Shepherds.

Jack relieved me at 0200 and I crawled into the two-person tent alongside Ange. I'd slept in some rough places in my life, so the hard metal hull didn't affect me. I was out in less than a minute.

TWELVE

I awoke suddenly to the sound of loud gunshots. Ange jolted awake beside me. Her eyes opened, and we shot up. We were both out of the tent with our hands wrapped around our pistols in seconds. The sounds had stopped by the time we stepped out into the dim early-morning light.

Jack stood at the stern, his compact Desert Eagle in one hand, the other holding a pair of binoculars up to his eyes. Atticus was standing beside him, his paws on the rail as he barked and peered inquisitively toward the source of the sounds.

"Heard three shots in all," Jack said before either of us could ask.

Sound travels well over water, and the sporadic low-elevation islands offer little resistance to passing sound waves. It makes it difficult to gauge how far away and from what direction a sound originated.

"I think it came from over there," Jack said, pointing southwest.

There was a layer of morning fog hovering over

106

the landscape. Piercing through the veil of white, we could just barely see the stretch of land that Jack was pointing at.

"Isn't that the island that Eli guy said he'd be staying at?" Ange said.

Just as the words left her lips, the still morning air was cut by a loud, sharp cry. It was high-pitched, but definitely a man's voice, and it boomed across the Glades for a few seconds before being silenced by two more gunshots.

"Holy shit," Jack said.

In an instant, I was at the bow, untying the line that kept us in place in the slow-moving river.

"Time to move, Jack!" I said.

He was already climbing into the control seat and starting up the engine. Ange unclipped the bungee cords, and we collapsed the two tents as Jack accelerated us into a sweeping turn, bringing us around to face the direction of the sounds. We barely managed to strap the gear down before Jack had us roaring at full speed. The sound was painful, and I snatched both our sets of earmuffs and we donned them as the water flew past us.

Ange and I kept our eyes forward, doing our best to examine the scene while blocking the billowing wind as we rocketed at over sixty knots. We could see Eli's airboat tied off to our right on the western side of the island. I kept my right hand gripping my Sig while my eyes scanned over the thick shoreline, looking for any sign of movement.

I caught a brief glance of the Watson Chickee to the southeast. The kayaks were gone, along with the tents. There was no sign of the four people we'd seen the day before. Jack motored around the tip of the small arrowhead-shaped island and pulled up

107

alongside Eli's airboat. I spotted what looked like a trail, and before Jack had shut off the engine, I vaulted the gap and landed on a small patch of dirt.

The engine died at my back. I yelled for Atticus to stay on the boat. Keeping my eyes forward, I moved as fast as I could along the path, heading toward the center of the island. Seconds later, I heard footsteps behind me. Looking back over my shoulder for a second, I saw Jack and Ange closing in with their weapons ready.

The ground was a messy tangle of roots and branches. Overhead was a solid canopy of green. In the early-morning light, the inner part of the island was shrouded in shadows, making it difficult to navigate the overgrown trail. At the center of the island was a cluster of cypress trees, and as I moved closer, I spotted a bright blue tarp, a bedroll with a blanket, and a folding chair in a small clearing.

Sweat covered my brow. It was already warm and humid. My heart raced as I raised my weapon, ready to take down a bad guy at a moment's notice.

When I moved within a few hundred feet of the clearing, I slowed and caught a whiff of a powerful stench. It was the raw, overbearing smell of gasoline. The fumes tore into my nostrils, catching me off guard as they dominated the fresh swampy air of the Glades.

Gunshots. Screams. Gasoline. What the hell's going on here?

I looked around, but it was difficult to see more than twenty feet through the thick brush surrounding me. Ange and Jack had caught up and were right on my heels. The three of us moved in, and when we reached the clearing, we spotted someone for the first time.

108

Eli lay bent over a thick tangle of roots. He had his back to us and wasn't moving. It was clearly him, given his uniquely small stature. He was also wearing the same clothes he'd been wearing the evening before.

I raised my Sig and stepped toward him cautiously. We'd made good time from the mouth of the river, reaching the center of the island less than five minutes after hearing the gunshots and scream. Whoever had fired off the rounds was still close by.

"Got you covered, Logan," Ange said. "Close in and see if he's breathing."

I nodded, lowered my Sig, and strode over to Eli. He was still alive. I could tell that before I'd touched him by observing the rising and lowering of his body. I wrapped an arm around him and carefully turned his body around to face me. I'd expected to find stains of dark red across his body, but I saw nothing. He looked fine but was breathing heavily.

His eyes were closed and his left arm was hidden beneath the thick brush beside us. For a moment, I thought he was stuck. Then his arm began to slide out. His eyes opened and his breathing relaxed in an instant. Before I knew what was happening, his hand appeared into view. He was holding his M1911 handgun.

I didn't have time to raise my Sig, didn't have time to wonder at his motives. All I could do was lunge toward his left hand as the barrel of his weapon arched toward me and his finger pulled the trigger. The sound was overwhelming. A loud and powerful boom that roared like thunder just a few feet from my face and rattled my eardrums. My head shook and my mind fell into a painful haze. I could hear nothing but a high-pitched ringing in my right ear as I continued to force Eli's gun hand toward the ground.

Using all my strength, I forced myself over him and slammed his hand hard, knocking the revolver loose before he could manage another squeeze of the trigger. He gritted his teeth, let out a grunt, and retaliated by throwing his right fist toward my face. I tilted my head back and felt only the graze of knuckles against my chin.

I let out a grunt of my own, then let him have it. A strong right, a pounding left, and then another right. I was stronger and more trained than he was, and after a few seconds, I'd crunched his face into a bloody pulp. He struggled to breathe, struggled to do anything but shake as I ripped his life away.

Soon his head dropped back, lifeless, and his eyes shot sideways. For a second I thought he was dead, then his eyes focused and I realized that he was looking at something.

No, not something. Someone.

My mind was still hazy and my ears still rang painfully from the gunshot. I focused my gaze on the thick foliage surrounding us and saw a large man standing a few hundred feet away. He was standing perfectly still, facing us.

It was hard to see him under the shaded canopy of the tall cypress trees, but he looked similar to the big guy who I'd tussled with the previous morning. He was big and husky and wore camo clothing from head to toe. He had a bandanna covering the bottom half of his face like some kind of Wild West bandit. His forehead looked strange, like it was covered in scars.

What drew most of my attention, however, was the silver object in his right hand. It was small—too small to be a pistol. And it was rectangular.

110

My eyes grew wide as the top part of the object hinged up in an instant. With the quick flick of his fingers, the killer sparked a small flame to life.

Gunshots. Screams. Gasoline. Fire.

The killer let the tiny glow flicker a few times, then dropped the Zippo. The moment it hit the ground, it ignited, setting the thick tangle of branches ablaze. I gasped as the flames spread, forming a circle that was quickly closing in around us.

The crazy asshole had led us into a trap.

THIRTEEN

With the flames racing around me, following a drenched trail of gasoline, I reached for my Sig. In less than a second, I had the sights raised toward where the killer had been standing, but he was gone. He'd vanished into the dark jungle around me.

Fire roared and smoke billowed around me. We had to move. We all had to get the hell out of there, and fast.

Jumping to my feet, I swung my leg and kicked Eli's left knee hard enough that I heard it crack over the scorching flames beside us. He yelled in pain, spitting out gobs of blood onto the dirt beside his face. I didn't know if I'd be making it out of there alive, but I knew for certain that Eli Hutt didn't stand a chance. He'd die right there. He'd sealed his fate when he'd tried to take us down.

"Logan!" I heard Ange scream over my ringing ears.

I whirled around with my Sig raised, expecting to see the killer once again. Instead, I saw Jack lying on

112

his back. Blood stained his gray tee shirt, and his face contorted in pain. Ange knelt beside him, trying to help him to his feet.

I sprinted over and dropped down beside my friend. He'd been shot, that much was clear. Fortunately, the bullet had only grazed his side just under his right armpit. But he was still bleeding out steadily and would need help getting to his feet.

"Damn, it hurts," he said, biting hard and wincing as I dropped down and wrapped an arm around him.

As we lifted him to his feet, Ange and I glanced over at the wall of fire that was just about to close in around us. I could feel the heat from the scorching flames as we helped Jack toward the trail back to the airboat. We struggled to reach it before the flames did but were too late. Like a slamming gate, the walls of fire connected, sealing us in a circle of intense heat. The dry summer plants, doused in gasoline, burst into flames and quickly spread out toward us. Waves of smoke grew thicker and thicker, making it difficult to breathe.

Looking forward, I saw a wall of flames at least five feet wide blocking our way back to the path. I coughed and lifted the neck of my shirt up over my nose and mouth to try and block out the choking smoke. I quickly ran through our limited options. We could make a run for it. At best we'd get through with second-degree burns. At worst, third-degree, or it was possible we wouldn't make it at all.

Time was running out as the flames roared around us. We needed to think of something.

I glanced over my shoulder at Eli's camp and got an idea.

"Hold Jack," I said. Before Ange could reply, I

shifted his weight, forcing her to hold him up. "I'll be right back!"

She and Jack both said something I couldn't hear over the ringing in my ears and the crackling of the flames. I sprinted back to the camp, snatched the blanket from the bedroll, and ran back to the others. Wool is naturally flame resistant and doesn't melt or stick to your skin when it burns.

Even in the few seconds it took me to run over and get back, the flames had spread significantly. When I reached them, I unfolded the blanket and stepped as close as I could to the heat without my skin getting seared. The blanket wouldn't guarantee our safe escape from the inferno, but it would sure help our chances.

"On the count of three, we sprint for it!" I said, helping Jack and Ange closer.

We could feel the heat growing in severity. We didn't have long. Maybe just a few more seconds before the flames took over and completely engulfed our little refuge.

"One... two... three!"

I tossed the blanket over the fire, creating a narrow path through the blaze. We took off into the opening with reckless abandon. The heat scorched our bodies, baking us like an intense oven as we passed through. After what felt like an eternity, we broke free on the other side and staggered to a stop on the overgrown trail.

We coughed and caught our breath as we pressed on, putting distance between us and the fire. I looked both Jack and Ange up and down. Our skin was red and I'd lost a few arm hairs, but we were alive. The wool had done its job well.

Ange glanced over at me, letting me know that

she was okay, then looked around. The killer was still close by and we were both ready to make him pay.

"You alright?" I said to Jack.

His head was down and he groaned.

"Shit, bro," he said. He shook his head and added, "At least I won't have to cauterize this thing."

We moved as fast as we could down the overgrown path toward the airboat. We kept our heads on a swivel and reached the water in under a minute. The flames continued to spread at our backs, and I knew that it was only a matter of minutes before the entire island went ablaze.

As we loaded Jack onto the airboat and prepared to start up the engine, I watched as two boats suddenly motored into view. The sound of the burning island and the ringing in my ears had kept me from noticing them earlier. One was heading straight for us, cruising around the northern tip of the island. The other was flying away from us, heading for an island-riddled bay east of the mouth of the Watson River.

It took only a brief glance at each to realize who they were. The guy hightailing it out of there was the killer who'd just started the forest fire. The boat heading toward us was Pete and his friend. When they reached us, Jack grabbed me by the shirt and struggled his upper body toward me.

"Go and get him, Logan," he said. "Take him down or he'll keep doing this."

He had the fire reflecting in his stern eyes. I knew he'd be right with me if he were able, but he needed help fast if he was going to keep from bleeding to death.

I turned to Ange.

"Can you—"

"Already on it," she said, grabbing a first aid kit from one of the bags.

"What the hell's going on here?" Pete yelled, his eyes scanning from us to the burning island behind us.

He shut off the engine and stepped to the port bow.

"No time to explain," I said. "I need you to take Jack back to Flamingo and get him help ASAP. He's been shot."

Ange and I helped Jack carefully onto the other boat. She dropped down beside him, ripped open a few bandages, and put pressure on his bleeding side.

"What are you gonna do?" Pete asked in a stern and authoritative voice.

I untied our boat and pointed northeast before plopping down into the control seat.

"I'm going after him," I said, matching his tone. "Atticus, hop over, boy," I added, motioning toward Pete's boat.

He looked at me in confusion, then reluctantly jumped over before I could repeat the order. As fast as I could, I started up the engine and accelerated away from the shoreline. Pete's friend, who'd helped Jack transition to their boat but hadn't spoken a word since they'd shown up, unexpectantly launched himself across the gap and landed on the starboard bow. I wanted to yell at him to jump back, to tell him that I could take care of this guy myself. But there wasn't any time to spare. Every second we sat still, the killer moved farther and farther away from us. It wouldn't be long before he vanished into the fog-veiled swamp, leaving us with nothing but a scorched island and a dead inside man to show for the violent and dangerous confrontation.

116

I took one last look at Ange before the fan reached full speed, propelling us over the water in a torrent of loud, powerful wind. She looked worried, and I could tell that she wanted to come with. But she needed to take care of Jack. I tilted my head back and gave her a brief reassuring nod before turning and bringing us up to full speed.

FOURTEEN

Within seconds, I had the high-powered airboat up to its max speed of just over fifty knots. We tore across the water, a loud booming rocket of power that caused the water and sporadic islands to fly by in a blur. I cast safety to the wind and chased down the killer with reckless abandon. In under a minute, he was in my sights.

I lined up the bow with the killer's boat and pressed forward. The massive engines of the former tour boat gave us a necessary advantage in our little game of cat and mouse. The killer's airboat was fast, but not fast enough. I followed him across a small bay and into the mouth of a narrow waterway that cut northeast.

I kept my breathing calm and steady as I held tight to the controls. My gaze remained locked on the boat ahead of us, my eyes narrowed. When we closed to within a few hundred feet, close enough to feel the powerful wind from his boat blowing into us, he cut a sudden hard left. It was fast and smooth and allowed him to sweep around a small mangrove island that lay dead ahead of us.

With no time to spare, I turned as well, letting off the gas to keep the boat from flipping and tumbling into a disastrous wreck. The hull groaned and skidded across the water like a skipped rock. Turning at that speed proved incredibly difficult, and it took me a few seconds to regain control and continue the arch around the small island.

Shit, this guy can pilot an airboat.

It was an understatement. He operated the craft like it was an extension of his own body rather than a machine. I had the faster boat, but it quickly became clear that it wouldn't matter in the cramped island-and-sharp-turn-riddled environment of the Glades. As I re-accelerated toward him and a tangle of waterways, I knew what I had to do.

I glanced at Pete's friend, who was kneeling and holding on to the railing just a few feet shy of the bow. He kept his head down and his eyes forward. Pete said that his name was Billy. He'd also told me that he was a Seminole, a man who grew up near the Glades. He was a tall guy, a few inches over my six-foot-two. He was lean and wiry and moved with incredible balance on the rapidly moving boat.

"Hey!" I yelled at the top of my lungs. He brushed aside his long black hair and looked back with squinted eyes. "Take over!"

I'd never met this guy, but I was willing to bet that he had more experience operating an airboat than I had. I'd also wager that I'd taken down more bad guys in my time, so the switch made sense. He didn't argue. Without a word, he strode over, plopped down, and took over the controls just as I sprang up.

It was like giving Dale Earnhardt Jr. the keys to

119

his favorite '67 Camaro. He operated the difficult craft with incredible speed and control, smoothly zipping around islands, cutting sharp turns, and avoiding objects in our path. It wasn't long before he was locked on our quarry and closing in fast.

I snatched my Sig from its holster, gripping it with my right hand while my left held on to the gunwale to keep myself from flying overboard.

I shot a quick glance back at Pete's friend. I didn't know this guy, didn't know his opinions on taking the law into your own hands and shooting down a bad guy without due process. Thankfully, he didn't protest when he saw my gun. Not that it would've mattered. I was going to take this guy out, and at that moment, I didn't give a damn about what the law had to say about it.

We stormed into a series of long, sweeping turns as the narrow channel zigzagged back and forth. The overgrown tangle of mangroves covering the passing muddy shorelines provided just enough cover for the killer to stay out of my view. When we finally reached somewhat of a straightaway, I took aim and fired.

Bullets struck the massive fan and engine, which provided cover where the killer sat at the control seat of his airboat. Sparks shot out as round after round struck metal. The killer ducked and turned to keep us behind him. I let out five rounds in all, and soon his engine started shooting out plumes of black smoke.

His engine was dying, and the fan propelling him away from us slowed. I watched him scramble at the controls, knowing that soon he'd be dead in the water and would be forced to reach for whatever weapon he had nearby. I wasn't gonna sit by and give him the opportunity to fight back. The moment his body came into view, I'd let him have it.

As Billy brought us around the killer's port side, the killer cut a sharp right to keep his body out of my sights. Just as we flew beside him, he turned sharply back to the left. We were both still traveling at over forty knots. His boat jerked toward us in a fraction of a second, his hull slamming against ours just as I managed to pull the trigger.

In a chaotic blur of screeching metal and roaring engines, the bow of his smaller boat crashed under ours, causing his boat to violently twist sideways and flip while we were jerked hard and launched into the air. The force of the collision nearly knocked me out of the boat as we jolted up and crashed down into the water. Water splashed over the side, and we spun out of control and flipped. The force hurled me from the bow, tossing me like a rag doll into the murky water.

My vision was blurry and dark as I twisted and thrashed. It felt like I'd been swept up by a massive crashing wave, and I couldn't tell what direction was up. I swam and my hands stuck into a layer of squishy mud. Digging my feet in, I sprang up out of the water and took in a much-needed breath of air.

Covered in mud and dirty water, I wiped my face and eyes and got my bearings. Right in front of me, just a few feet away, was the muddy shoreline of a small island that I hadn't noticed before. After landing and flipping, our airboat had continued forward, crashing out of control into the island and leveling a broken path in the dense mangroves. The wrecked airboat was fifty feet away from me, lying upside down in a swampy bog of seagrass. Billy was nowhere to be found.

Turning around, I scanned the other boat, which was on its side and half-submerged. I saw no sign of the killer either, but knew he had to be there. I'd hit him before we'd collided, I was sure of it. But I wasn't sure whether it was a fatal blow.

I reached for my waistband to grab my Sig and finish the job, but it wasn't there. I remembered that I'd been holding it when we'd crashed—it must have flown out of my hand during the chaos. It didn't matter. I still had my knife, and as long as I could reach him before he grabbed a weapon, I wouldn't need a firearm to take him out.

"Help!" I heard a voice cry out from behind me.

I turned around, facing the island and the wrecked airboat, but couldn't see any movement.

"Help! I'm stuck!" I heard the same voice call out again.

It was Billy.

Without hesitating, I moved as quickly as I could up onto the muddy shoreline, heading for the wrecked airboat. I scanned back and forth as I moved, keeping a sharp eye out for him.

He yelled for help a few more times, but his words were a struggle. He gurgled and spat. Sounded like he was drowning.

When I reached the airboat, I saw Billy lying on his back in the mud and water. The engine and fan had been completely ripped off, and the starboard gunwale was jammed into his chest, forcing his upper body a few inches underwater. With the massive airboat weighing him down, he had to struggle and force his body up just to get a much-needed breath.

I ran over as fast as I could through the thick tangle of branches, bent down beside him, and dug my fingers under the metal.

"One…two…three!" I yelled.

With all my strength, I pressed my legs down

while pulling up with my arms. I grunted and my muscles screamed as I brought the edge up high enough for Billy to shimmy out of the water and mud. Just as his feet were clear, I let go, causing the boat to splash down in front of me.

We were both breathing heavily as I moved over beside him, making sure he was okay.

"Anything broken?" I said, checking him over.

He coughed and spat out muddy water.

"Shoulder hurts like hell," he said. "But I don't think so."

I reached down and helped him to his feet. Turning around, I looked back at the killer's airboat, which was still resting half-sunk in the water just offshore from the island.

"You see where he went?" Billy asked, staggering in front of me.

"No," I said. "Haven't seen him since he decided to go kamikaze on us."

We moved to the shore and looked around. My adrenaline was still pumping from the chase and crash. I expected the killer to rise up from around his wrecked boat at any moment, but it didn't happen. I hoped that he'd drowned, that I'd struck him with a 9mm round and he'd been unable to reach the surface. But I always liked to be prepared for the worst. I'd only encountered him twice, but it was clear from those interactions that this wasn't your ordinary bad guy. Just as Pete had predicted a few days earlier at his restaurant, this guy was tough as nails and not someone to be underestimated.

Just as I turned to head back for our airboat to see if I could find my spare Sig and binoculars, I heard sloshing in the water right around an overhanging cluster of mangroves. Boots squished and sucked in the mud. I whirled back just in time to see a man appear around the corner. He had a compound bow in his hands, an arrow nocked and pulled back, aimed straight at us.

It was Hank Boggs. The jerk who'd gotten in my face the previous afternoon at Flamingo.

He wore a backward camo ball cap, and his thick black beard covered most of his face. Other than the hat, he looked exactly how he had when we'd had our hot-blooded conversation the previous day at Flamingo. His hip boots were covered in mud, and he had a layer of sweat on his brow. He eyed us with a focused gaze. Didn't look angry or flustered.

I calculated how fast I could snag my new hunting knife, tuck to the side, and fling it in his direction. But there was no chance of it. He was too experienced, and I'd be a damn kabob before I could even have the blade clear of the sheath.

Suddenly, I heard a loud shuffling and a growl behind me. An instant later, Hank released the arrow. The carbon fiber arms shot out, snapping the line and sending the arrow straight toward us. In a strong whoosh of air, the arrow zipped right by us and struck flesh. But it wasn't our flesh. I quickly spun around and watched as a massive alligator hissed and groaned. The arrow's sharp broadhead jammed into its thick skin. Blood oozed out from its mouth and dripped down its bottom row of sharp teeth.

It was just a few feet away from Billy and me. Angered and in pain from the blow, it retreated into a pool of murky water and struggled its way out of sight.

I turned back to Hank. He'd lowered his bow but was watching the prehistoric predator with cautious eyes. I couldn't believe what had just happened.

124

Seeing him standing with the bow raised and an arrow aimed at us, I'd thought we were done for sure. I was just about to thank him when he beat me to words.

"That's the second time in two days you scared off one of my hogs, Dodge," he said. Then he glanced over at my newfound companion and added, "Billy Thatcher. You two know each other?"

"No," Billy said.

"An introduction was tabled on account of that boat's owner," I added and pointed out over the water.

Hank looked over at the barely floating airboat and nodded.

"He jumped ship while crashing into you," Hank said. "Took off north toward that shoreline." He pointed at a stretch of muddy shore barely visible through a light veil of fog. "He had an arm across his chest. Looked injured."

Shit, I thought.

But it sure as hell figured. It would've been far too easy had he just drowned like a normal person.

"You see where he went after that?" I asked.

Hank shook his head. "Didn't see anything else. I came here as fast as I could when I heard Billy calling for help."

I nodded, turned around, and strode back to the upside-down airboat. Crawling under, I pulled out all of the bags I could reach. I unzipped my waterproof bag, pulled out my extra Sig, and holstered it under the right side of my drenched waistband. Then I loaded up some provisions, camping gear, and extra ammunition. I didn't know how long we'd be tracking this guy, and I wanted to be prepared. We had to bear in mind that the other guy I'd run into yesterday was also still at large.

"I can carry that," Billy said, extending a hand toward one of the backpacks in front of me.

I nodded and held it up to him with my left hand.

"Logan Dodge," I said, extending my right.

He shook it and replied, "Billy Thatcher."

"Well, Billy, you up for a hunt?"

He gave me an expression that was almost a smile. I guessed it was about as close to one as I was gonna get. I rose to my feet, strapped on my bag, and headed back to the shoreline alongside him.

"You know, for a second I thought you were about to try and use me for target practice," I said to Hank, who was lighting up a Perla cigar.

It was the second time in two days that an arrow had flown inches away from me at over three hundred feet per second. Even I felt like I was pushing my luck.

"I may be a mean cuss, Dodge," he said, breathing in to light the end in a bright red ember, then exhaling smoke, "but I ain't no murderer. And try?" He laughed. "If I'd wanted you dead, you'd be in that gator's mouth right now."

"Well, it isn't a hog, but if you can find it I'm sure you can make good use of the meat," I said. "I'm sure Mitch won't mind that they aren't in season."

"Those ferocious predators are always in season," he rebutted.

"Mind if I ask another favor?" I said, raising my thumb like a hitchhiker and nodding in the direction the killer had gone.

"Sure beats a swim," he said. "Believe it or not, that gator that just tried to make you guys a snack wasn't the only one in here. My boat's just around the corner. I'll have you both over there in no time."

126

FIFTEEN

We stepped off Hank's skiff and onto a muddy shoreline covered in thickets. In just a few seconds, we spotted a trail of boot prints in the mud. They pointed north, inland through the thick green vegetation.

"I'll contact Mitch," Hank said. "See if he can send out a group to salvage the boats." He took a deep, long drag of his cigarette, then let it all out and wiped the sweat from his brow with his shirtsleeve. "Good luck."

I thanked him and he hit the gas, motoring back over to the small island.

Without a word, Billy and I moved inland, following a trail of occasional prints and broken branches. For a quarter mile, we kept our weapons in hand, expecting our injured enemy to jump out at any moment. We moved as quickly as could be expected through the difficult landscape, tangles of branches and vines littering an expanse of knee-deep, murky water.

After a mile, I thought we'd lost the killer's trail, but Billy assured me we still had him. He pointed out minuscule details, subtle changes to the natural order that only a man with a lifetime of experience in the swamp could notice. I didn't know anything about him, but I was glad to have him along. My knowledge of the Glades was minimal at best, consisting of a combination of things I'd learned during a small handful of trips to hunt pythons and an episode of *Man vs. Wild*.

In the silence of the hunt, I thought about Eli Hutt: a man the head ranger Mitch had seemingly trusted, who it turned out had been working with the killers. Hell, he was one of the killers. First one bad guy and now three. I shook my head and wondered how big this sadistic operation was. The word *motive* kept jumping into my mind. What kind of motive would create such a scheme? Were all these guys just in it for the cruel, sick pleasure of causing harm?

Then my mind raced back to what Ange had found in the sunken dinghy. A bag of coke. Money. Money and the protection of it. That had to be the motive. It explained why they'd killed the Shepherds, and it explained why they were trying to off us as well. We were getting in the way of their longstanding business.

Maybe you can offer your damn gator jerky to the devil, I thought as I pictured Eli's broken body. *He might give you a fine piece of real estate right on the lake of fire.*

Maybe Mitch was also working with them. Maybe this rabbit hole went deeper than we could've possibly imagined upon first glance. Regardless, I was determined to get to the bottom of it. And the only way to do that would be to track and take down the big fat killer who'd tried to wring my neck yesterday and burn me to death today.

After two hours of trekking through the unfriendly terrain, we reached a small patch of dry land covered in high cypress trees. The sun had risen, burning off the morning fog with ease and bleeding through the canopy surrounding us. My clothes were still wet and muddy. They caked to my body as the temperature quickly soared, and beads of sweat began to form on my exposed skin.

"Stay here," Billy said. They were the first words he'd spoken in over an hour. He motioned toward a vine-covered water oak tree beside us and added, "I'm gonna climb up and have a look around."

I slid off my backpack, unzipped the main compartment, and grabbed my monocular.

"Here," I said, handing it to him.

He nodded, then wrapped the string around his neck and rose up into the tree like a professional climber. I took a quick look around, drank from my canteen, then grabbed my GPS and sat phone. Powering up the GPS, I saw that we'd traveled just over four miles through the swamps.

While Billy climbed, I made a quick call to Ange. Even though I knew it wasn't a lethal wound, I was worried about Jack and I wanted to make sure he was alright.

"Where are you?" Ange asked. "Are you alright?"

"I'm fine," I said. "I'd be better if I hadn't been part of a swamp rage airboat collision."

"What?"

"Nothing. The killer got away from us, but we're on his trail. How's Jack?"

"Oh, you know that crazy islander," Ange said.

"He was begging for us to turn around and go help you the whole ride back. He'll have a decent scar, but no serious damage. Grazed by a forty-five—he's one lucky beach bum."

I gave her a quick rundown of what had happened after we'd taken off after the killer. She quickly asked what she could do to help. She was at Flamingo and could be across Whitewater in her Cessna in minutes if need be.

"You alright, Ange? You sound almost worried."

"Worried? Why should I be? My newlywed husband is marching through a dangerous swamp, tracking down a well-known serial killer, with a complete stranger as his companion."

I paused a moment.

"Ange, this isn't exactly my first time in a dangerous situation. You of all people know that."

"I do know that. I'd just feel a lot better if I was at your side."

She was right. No matter how many times I'd tried to protect her over the years, she usually ended up being the one to save me.

I sighed and said, "We're miles away from a suitable LZ for the bird. And there are no nearby tributaries wide enough to get a boat up. I'll call you as soon as we reach one. I promise."

"Alright, well, in the meantime I'd like updates on your position. Coordinates wherever you guys make camp tonight."

"As you wish," I said, quoting a favorite movie of ours.

She laughed and reminded me that if I wanted a buttercup, I should've checked the local mall. She was more of a Lara Croft.

After a few *I love you*s, we both hung up.

"See anything?" I said, glancing up at Billy.

He was holding on to a thick branch and leaning out, peering through my monocular.

"Not yet," he replied.

I took the time to make a second call.

"Anything come up on the prints?" I asked Scott Cooper when he picked up on the second ring.

"No, but you're not going to believe this," he said enthusiastically. He paused a moment, like an actor stretching the suspense. "After the prints came up empty in the database, I decided to try and learn something about the knife. It's obviously old and it's well made, so it caused me to wonder. The markings on the hilt had been scratched off, but I got a few guys down at the forensics lab to examine it closely, and they found a partially worn set of initials. Turns out it has quite the history. It belonged to Brigadier General Joseph Finegan, an Irishman who fought for the Confederates during the Civil War. Finegan died in 1885 in Rutledge, Florida." He paused a moment, letting it all sink in. "But that isn't the half of it. That knife was stolen during a bank robbery over ten years ago in Fort Meyers."

"A bank robbery?" I said, stroking my chin. "They have any suspects?"

"Yeah. Their faces were concealed while in the bank, but further investigation revealed that they were the Harlan brothers."

I thought for a moment, but the name didn't ring any bells.

"What can you tell me about those two brothers?"

"There's three of them, actually," Scott said. "And I can tell you that they're all supposed to be dead. The file says that while making their escape,

131

they drove off the Wilson Pigott bridge, into the Caloosahatchee River. Their bodies were never recovered, not uncommon in this part of the country."

Billy dropped down from the tree, landing softly beside me. When I turned to look at him, I realized that he was watching and listening intently to my conversation.

"And let me guess, none of the money they stole was ever recovered either?" I said.

"Looks like the local authorities wanted to clean up the mess and move on as quickly and easily as possible. We both know how that goes."

"You got pictures of these guys?"

"Have their mug shots and info on the screen now. The bank robbery wasn't any of their first times getting into trouble with the law."

"Don't tell me," I said. "About my height. Three hundred pounds. White skin, dark hair, double chins, faces like angry pit bulls."

He sighed. "Looks like you've got a few ghosts on your hands. Where you at now?"

"North of Whitewater. A few miles west of Watson River. Following the trail of one of the brothers."

"Alright," Scott said. "Keep me updated. And let me know when you need me to come down there and take care of business."

I laughed. "I wouldn't want you to get your suit dirty, Senator."

"Scratch that," he said. "I'll head down there, show you who's still the boss, then I'll take care of business."

That one caused my lips to transform into a smile. Scott was one of the most competitive guys I'd ever met. It had caused us to butt heads years ago, but

132

our similar nature had soon led to a strong friendship.

"You mind sending over their mug shots to my phone?"

"Already done," he said. "And I sent it over to Ange as well, which is good, 'cause it sounds like you probably don't have service."

"Thanks for the help, Scottie," I said.

When I ended the call, I turned and saw Billy standing stoically and staring ahead into the swamp. I moved over beside him, offering him the other canteen of water.

"What did he say about the Harlan brothers?" Billy asked.

He unscrewed the cap and took a few swigs.

"You know them?" I said, raising an eyebrow at him.

"Their family's been living here for generations. Can't say anyone missed them when they died. Been over ten years." He shook his head and added, "They were always a bad bunch. Moonshiners, poachers, thieves. Guess it figures they decided to add murderers to their resumes."

I took another drink myself, then stowed my GPS and sat phone.

"You see anything up there?"

He nodded.

"He's about a mile ahead of us. Moving pretty good for an injured guy. The mangrove forest opens up to the river of grass prairies and hammocks half a mile north of here."

"Any idea where he could be heading?"

He shook his head.

"No. But he's keeping a relatively straight line. We're running parallel to Watson. It flows a few miles to the east."

I tore open a few protein bars, which we both downed quickly. Neither of us had eaten anything since the previous day, and navigating through the Glades works up your appetite quick. After taking a few more swigs of water, we gathered our gear and continued our hunt. It was a slow trek through shallow water and tangles of branches for half a mile before the canopies opened up, revealing a never-ending expanse of grass and sporadic clusters of hammocks. In the southern United States, and especially in Florida, the word hammock isn't only used to define a swinging bed of fabric. It's also to describe a fertile area that's characterized by hardwood trees and deep humus-rich soil.

Looking out over the landscape, it's easy to see why Billy referred to the Glades as a river of grass.

"It's a sixty-mile-wide river," he said while we trekked. "All the water you see is moving south. It's a snail's pace, though. Only a hundred feet or so every twenty-four hours."

Before stepping out of the foliage and into the grass, Billy bent a few pop ash saplings and cut them free with his knife.

"Walking sticks?" I asked.

"Not exactly."

He splashed down into a shallow bog, moving right up to the outer wall of tall sawgrass.

"This grass will cut you to shreds," he said. He held out one of the sticks horizontally and pushed it against the grass, causing it to bow away from him. "Use the stick to keep it off you."

He handed me the other stick and we pressed on through the mud and thick grassland, following the faint trail left behind by our quarry. The hours dragged on and the temperature continued to rise as

134

the sun migrated directly overhead. It was difficult to see over the tall grass, and everywhere we turned looked the same.

In my time in the SEALs and the years I'd spent as a mercenary, I'd engaged enemies in every terrain under the sun. Dense jungles, arid deserts, freezing tundras. But the Glades are something different altogether. A special breed of never-ending swamps that gives a new definition to the term *difficult terrain*.

It was the rainy season, and it was living up to its title. It poured in thick sheets for minutes at a time, soaking us along with our gear before moving on. The heat was stifling, and the humidity made it difficult to breathe. Mosquitoes swarmed like black clouds, along with an ensemble of other pesky insects including horseflies, sand flies or no-see-ums, and chiggers.

I'd always preferred going to battle in unforgiving environments. Rough terrain and bad weather dampen morale, so if you can keep yourself together and embrace it, you have an advantage over your enemy. But it was different this time around, I reminded myself. The guy we were chasing not only embraced the southern Florida swamp, he called it home. He was the type of guy who was probably more comfortable right here in the heart of the Glades than anywhere else in the world. An anomaly. A modern-day Daniel Boone with a twisted murdering side.

I couldn't believe that he was managing to keep his distance from us. Especially considering that he was injured. I was sure that I'd shot him before we crashed, and Hank had said that he'd looked injured when he took off. But maybe he wasn't injured. Maybe we were wrong. Regardless, we were chasing either the roughest man alive or some kind of demon.

For what felt like the hundredth time since we'd started out that morning, I grabbed my bug spray and drenched what little of our skin was exposed. Without the hundred-percent DEET, I'd have been covered in itchy red spots just minutes into the trek.

We kept silent for most of the day. Occasionally I'd ask him about a particular stretch of landscape or a unique plant that was foreign to me. We'd only known each other for half of a day, but I liked Billy. He didn't talk a lot, which I'd take any day over someone who couldn't stop running their mouth. He also didn't complain. The entire day in the heat and the wet and the bugs, he never once complained.

It wasn't until late afternoon that we finally felt like we were closing in on the killer. Billy was a better tracker than I was, and he led us up onto a large hammock that was covered in cypress and water oak. As we moved into its interior, Billy pointed at a cluster of grapefruit trees. Their fruits were ripe, so we grabbed and broke into a few. The citrus liquid was delicious and fresh. I grabbed two more and ate while we walked.

"I didn't know grapefruit grew here," I said.

Billy nodded and swallowed a bite.

"It's not indigenous," he said. "The plants were brought down by my ancestors. The Seminole tribe was forced to live here in the Glades after our land was taken."

He had a naturally stoic tone, but it turned agitated as he mentioned his tribe's history. I didn't know much about the native people of Florida, but I knew that, like most Native Americans, they were generally treated terribly by European settlers.

"Stop!" Billy said, raising a hand. I froze just a

step behind him, watched as he bent down and examined a small stretch of dirt. "He's close."

I knelt down beside him and examined the ground. I could see boot prints, but there was more than one set and they were heading in different directions.

"How can you tell?"

He pointed, hovering his right index finger inches over the indentations in the dirt.

"He's trying to divert us," he said. "To put us on a fake trail. It can mean only one thing: he's grown weary. Or perhaps he's reached his destination. But either way, I'm confident that he's within half a mile of us right now."

Some destination, I thought.

I looked around at nothing but dirt patches and thick hardwood jungle surrounded by endless marsh and dense grasslands. My money was on his first explanation. We'd moved fast and had caught up to him. If he was still close by, it meant that he was most likely planning to ambush us. I tried to put myself into his shoes, into the mind of a serial killer. If I was a serial killer on the run in the Glades with two men after me, I'd try and take them out when the odds were most in my favor. I'd attack them when they were most vulnerable. In the middle of the night, while they were in a deep sleep.

I looked up at the sky. The sun was nearing the horizon. Within the hour, darkness would fall across the swamp.

"We should set up camp," I said.

Billy looked at me like I was crazy.

"I know you have ears, Logan," he said. "I just told you that the killer's close by. If we set up camp, he'll know about it. Hell, he's probably waiting for

137

it."

"Exactly," I declared. "I've underestimated this guy. Now, I want him to underestimate us."

He stared at me, then glanced away, his confusion fading slightly.

"We've been chasing him all day," I added, clarifying my plan. "It's time we let this predator come to us."

SIXTEEN

Angelina sat in the Baia's galley, staring intently at the laptop screen in front of her. She'd spoken with Scott Cooper just an hour earlier and he'd sent over a file containing the mug shots and basic rap sheets of three men. Buck, Dale, and Jeb Harlan. All three were supposed to be dead.

She looked over their files, then turned her attention back to the charts and maps.

So many incidents near this one river, she thought as she pointed to the mouth of the Watson River. *One river among thousands of tributaries littering the Glades.*

She leaned back into the cushioned half-moon seat. Grabbing a chilled can of coconut water, she took a few sips, then set it beside her. As she drew her hand back, it grazed her backpack and she remembered that the coke was still inside. Rising to her feet, she stepped into the main cabin and locked it up in the safe. They'd decided to continue keeping the drug's existence among themselves and not tell the authorities. Logan had thought it best, seeing as how they didn't know how deep the trafficking operation went. Maybe the killers had someone on the inside of the law, covering them and taking a cut.

When she sat back down in the galley, she thought about the powdery drug.

Like Logan, she thought that the Harlan brothers must have been selling it, that they'd most likely turned to drugs out of desperation.

But how did they distribute it? And how had they remained hidden all these years?

They'd spent half an hour flying their drone over the river, filming and scanning everything in view. They hadn't seen so much as a rustic tin roof. Not even the faintest sign of a long-term dwelling.

She kept at it, going over maps and the footage they'd shot of the Watson River.

Suddenly, Atticus stormed into the galley from the main cabin and rushed to the topside door. He wagged his tail and glanced back at Ange.

"You hear something, boy?" she said, walking over and patting the top of his head.

She listened intently for a few seconds and heard footsteps heading down the dock. Opening the door and stepping up into the cockpit, she saw Jack flip-flopping toward the Baia.

"Any news?" she asked.

His head popped up in surprise, then he relaxed a little.

"Don't scare me like that, sheesh," he said. When he reached the port gunwale, he added, "Dial down the ninja assassin movements, will ya?"

She laughed and helped him aboard, though he didn't really need it. The bullet had only grazed him, and Jack looked as strong and wiry as ever.

"Sorry, didn't mean to make you wet your pants."

"Hey, they were already wet."

She smiled.

"Well? You guys learn anything over at the station?"

Jack had been with Mitch and Pete over at the ranger station for the past couple of hours.

"Fire didn't spread, but that island's a wasteland now," he said. "Not much left of Eli Hutt. They hauled the airboat back. It was pretty messed up. The killer's airboat is done for, though. They said it was sunk in eight feet when they arrived."

"That's alright," Ange said. "The Harlan brothers won't be needing it soon."

Jack paused a moment as Atticus wagged his happy tail against his leg.

"Harlan brothers?" he said with raised eyebrows.

Ange motioned toward the Baia's galley.

"Come on down," she said. "We should get Pete in on this too. We've got some good new intel."

They called Pete, and the three of them headed back down into the galley. Ange showed them the mug shots and gave them a quick update on Logan and Billy.

"Damn," Jack said as he looked over the photos. "These guys are even uglier up close."

"No kidding," Pete said, mentioning that they could be long-lost relatives of Jabba the Hutt.

They read over the rap sheets. They were long and contained incidents that dated back to when they were young.

Ange rubbed her eyes and leaned back into the seat around the dinette. It was getting late. She'd been staring at screens and downing coffee all day and her body was urging her to call it quits.

"What's that?" Jack said.

Ange turned around and saw that he was staring at the laptop screen. The monitor was still playing the drone's footage on a loop. The same thirty minutes of never-ending nothingness that she'd been watching over and over all night.

Ange stepped toward Jack and leaned in to look at the screen.

"What's what?" she said.

Jack leaned forward, pointing at the screen.

"Ah, it's gone now." He looked down at the keyboard in confusion. Computers weren't his thing. That was his nephew's department. "Can you rewind this thing?"

Ange extended a hand, brought the footage back thirty seconds, then pressed play.

"Okay, pause it at 24:13 on the time stamp," Jack said.

Fifteen seconds later, Ange paused the screen.

Jack stared closely, tilting his head slightly. Ange and Pete both looked closer too but couldn't see anything unusual. Just a filthy river surrounded by a sea of green.

"You see right there?" Jack said. "Where the river forks?"

He pointed at the screen and Ange nodded. It still didn't strike her as anything but ordinary. The Watson River branched off hundreds of times, extending like tangled tree roots up into the swamp.

Jack's mouth dropped open and he narrowed his gaze even more. For a second, Ange thought that their conch charter captain friend had gone off the deep end.

Or maybe he hit his head too hard after getting

142

shot.

Martha at the ranger station had given him some painkillers to dull the pain. Ange considered that delirium might have been one of the side effects.

She rose up, grabbed a bottled water from the fridge, then extended it to Jack.

"Here," she said. "You're probably dehydrated. And you should get some rest. It's been a long day."

The bottle hung in the air right in front of Jack for a few seconds. If he'd heard her, he didn't show it.

"Jack, you—"

"This could be it!" Jack smiled broadly, then laughed a little before wincing and placing a hand on his side. "Ah, that one hurt."

"Okay, time for you to go to bed, crazy," Ange said, no longer playing it subtle.

Instead of grabbing the bottle, he wrapped his hand around her wrist and pulled her in softly.

"Look, Ange," he said. "This island right here."

He pointed at a small island right beside where the river forked.

"Look closely at the northwestern shore," he added.

She looked, more to humor him than anything else. There wasn't anything there. It was just a normal island and a normal muddy bank. Then, she saw it.

"Holy crap," she said. Now it was her mouth's turn to drop open. "Is that what I—"

"Yes," Jack declared. "That's exactly what we think it is."

The drone had been flying a hundred feet up, so the picture wasn't perfect. But Ange focused in on the image and saw a figure standing right where the canopy line met the muddy shore. A human figure. It appeared in view for only a few seconds before

143

jerking away, disappearing under the thick tree canopy.

Pete patted Jack on the back and said, "I knew you weren't crazy. Well, not that crazy anyway."

"Jack, how in the hell did you see that?"

"Got twenty-fifteen," he said with a grin.

They played the short clip over and over, their faces glued just inches away from the screen.

"The question is," Pete said, "where the hell is his boat? He's nearly four miles up Watson. Fifteen miles from the nearest service and ten miles from the nearest road. Nobody just goes off hiking that far into this terrain. Nobody reaches places like that without a boat."

"Is it possible he pulled it up onto the shore?" Ange asked. "Maybe we just can't see it."

"Most likely," Jack said.

"You ever see someone in the Glades pull their boat up onto a mangrove-infested shoreline?" Pete said. "No. Nobody does that because it's damn near impossible. They all tie off and let it float. The only reason that I can think of why someone wouldn't do that in the damn near heart of the Glades is if they didn't want to be seen. If they were in hiding."

Ange nodded, thinking over his words intently.

"Makes sense," she said. "And he hid from view just as the drone flew overhead."

"Exactly," Pete said. He shook his head and added, "I'm not sure what's on this island, but I think we need to head over there and take a look."

Ange paused the footage once again and stared intently at the human figure. Yes, heading over to the island was the obvious course of action. But if it turned out to be the Harlan brothers' hideout, she'd do a hell of a lot more than just have a look around.

144

SEVENTEEN

After ten minutes of scouring the island, keeping a sharp eye out for the killer, we found a suitable site. There was a clearing right beside a large gumbo-limbo tree with thick branches that sprouted out in all directions. While I went to work setting up our decoy camp, Billy gathered branches and began constructing our real camp ten feet up in the tree.

"Watch your step over there," Billy said, motioning toward a muddy bog just twenty feet from the base of the tree. "It's a sinkhole. Water erodes the limestone and creates a pocket that fills with mud and water. Some are big enough to swallow small off-road vehicles. I've seen it before."

I made a quick mental note, then went back to work. In just a few minutes, I had the tent and sleeping bags in place. I collected rocks, placing them in a circle to form a firepit, then started up a fire using dried branches, moss, and a little help from my lighter. Once the fire was crackling and burning thicker branches, I helped Billy finish the shelter. Not that he needed my help. He was almost finished by the time I offered to lend a hand.

There was a decent-sized platform of pop ash branches with a thatched roof. We found a few young sabal palm trees nearby. Also known as cabbage palm, they're the state tree of Florida, and we cut out a handful of long green fronds to use for bedding. After a few more finishing touches, the improvised shelter was complete.

I was thoroughly impressed by his survival skills. I'd never seen a better makeshift shelter, and he'd built it in just over an hour.

"Bear Grylls would be proud," I said.

I smiled slightly, but apparently Billy either didn't get the reference or he was too focused on the task at hand to even notice my comment.

By the time we finished, the sun was dropping over the horizon, sending sporadic streaks of light through the foliage surrounding us. As the air cooled, the bug population increased dramatically. Fortunately, the smoke from the fire helped keep them away, and we still had plenty of lifesaving DEET left.

As darkness fell over the swamp, we ate a quick meal of Meals Ready to Eat, or MREs as they're called. They were a common source of food during missions while I was in the Navy. The internal chemistry doesn't require a heat source. All you have to do is add water, and within a few minutes, you have a hot meal. Though many people complain about their taste, I'd always enjoyed them. I think it's because my dad had always packed them on camping trips when I was young.

I threw a few big logs on the fire, then we climbed up into our shelter in the gumbo-limbo tree. I had my Sig loaded up with a full magazine and holstered. To keep an eye out for the killer, I used my night vision monocular to scan the dark around us. Tangles of vines spun their way up the trunk and branches. The canopy was so thick that we could barely see the late-evening sky overhead. It would provide sufficient cover from the moonlight as we waited for our prey to make his move.

With the coming of the night, the marshy landscape around us transformed as an orchestra of sounds filled the air. Crickets, some of the loudest I'd ever heard, belted out chirps relentlessly. A handful of frogs joined in with croaks coming from all over the small island. Owls and various other birds provided occasional hoos and melodies. Toward the shore, we heard the occasional rustling and splashing of larger, more dangerous animals.

"The gators prefer to hunt at night," Billy said, after a particularly large splash. "Too hot for them in the day. When the summer sun's up, they spend a lot of their time in deeper waters to keep cool."

After an hour, we decided to take short turns trying to get some sleep. After years of sleeping wherever I could, I'd developed the ability to catch some z's just about anywhere. I've even dozed off while standing up a few times.

Two hours into our alternate watches, I awoke and felt a change in the air. Looking up at the night sky, I saw that it was even darker than it'd been before. What little silver light from the moon had trickled through the dense canopy earlier was now extinguished.

"We're about to get wet again," Billy whispered.

As if his words had summoned Mother Nature, roaring thunder shook the still air. Cracks of lightning followed, bolting down from the heavens and illuminating the darkness in sporadic flashes. It was just before midnight when black clouds swept overhead, covering most of the night sky. I felt the low-pressure air and heard a few warning raindrops slap against the leaves overhead, then all hell broke loose.

In much of the world, rain builds up steadily. In tropical environments, however, rain has a tendency to build up about as steadily as a shower when you twist the knob. One second you're dry, the next you're being drenched by a torrential downpour.

A waterfall of massive raindrops fell straight down, sliding off the leaves overhead and splashing into our bodies. The roof Billy had made worked nicely, but he'd been short on time and it was far from perfect. Within seconds, water started dripping down the bill of my Rubio Charters ball cap.

As quickly as the rains had descended, they were gone. The humid air returned as the clouds swept by, leaving the soaked earth and moving on to the north. I removed my hat, shook the water off, then wiped a combination of water and sweat from my brow. Gradually, the sounds of life returned around us and we resumed our shifts.

Just after 0230, I heard footsteps at my six. At first, I thought it could be a deer or a hog, but they were slow and heavy. Too heavy for any mammal in the Glades, and they didn't crunch over the leaf-covered landscape below like a gator would.

Slowly and silently, I shifted my body around and lifted my monocular up over my right eye. I'd recently upgraded to a new model. It was less grainy than the previous one I'd used and allowed me to zoom in farther. Staring into the thick brush around

148

us, I heard a footstep again and focused on the large figure of a man standing roughly fifty feet behind us. He stood perfectly still, his glowing eyes locked on our trap of a camp on the ground below.

Wanting to wake Billy before our prey got too close, I nudged him softly. His eyes sprang open and he tilted his head slowly.

"He's here," I whispered. I motioned in the killer's direction and added, "Your nine o'clock. Fifty feet. Right beside that stump."

He shifted his body, angled his head, and focused his eyes. After just a few seconds of searching, he nodded.

"What's the play?" he asked.

I thought for a second, then moved my head even closer to Billy's right ear.

"We wait until he's close," I said. "We injure him, disarm him, then get him to talk."

Billy nodded, grabbed his Springfield XD handgun from his waistband. I followed suit, gripping my Sig with my right hand and pulling it out.

Both armed, we fell perfectly silent and listened as the killer approached. His movements were impressively quiet for a guy his size. He stepped with ease over roots, under branches, and between closely knit trunks. It didn't surprise me. If he was one of the Harlan brothers, it meant that he'd been living on the run, probably hunting down most of his food, for over ten years.

Billy and I kept frozen as statues. We were both ready, just in case the killer spotted us up in the tree, to take him out in an instant.

He moved right into the camp below us, his boots landing softly the dirt with every step. He had his compound bow strapped to his back, and in his right hand, he clutched what looked like a sawed-off shotgun.

His eyes were glued to the tent as he shuffled slowly along the back side of it. I'd strapped the rain fly down, so he bent over, trying to catch a peek inside. Standing tall again, he lifted the shotgun, gripped it with two hands, and took aim. Just as we'd expected, this asshole was planning to take us both out in our sleep. With one pull of the trigger, he'd send a spray of lead pellets at over a thousand feet per second. Anything inside the tent would be riddled and mangled to pieces, including our flesh if we had been inside.

I raised my Sig slowly, aiming it straight at his hands. Lining up the sights, I let out my breath calmly and pulled the trigger. The 9mm round exploded from the chamber, flashing as the powder ignited and shocking the still evening air. It struck the top of the killer's right hand, tearing through flesh and spraying out blood and bone. The round easily broke all the way free and rattled against the wooden stock of the sawed-off shotgun.

He yelled in pain as the weapon broke from his grasp, spinning and falling harmlessly to the dirt at his feet. He brought his mangled hand against his chest and bent forward, wincing and gritting his teeth as the pain shot through his body.

He jerked his body around, stared into the dark jungle surrounding him. His left hand was pressed against his right. Blood flowed out and his hand shook. The sound of gunfire had caused every bug and critter nearby to fall silent, allowing us to hear every sound the guy made.

"What the fuck," he said, grunting the words out.

His head moved back and forth as he searched

for his attacker. After a few seconds, he directed his gaze up. He stared straight at us for a few seconds. Billy and I both had our weapons locked right on him.

He grunted again, turned around. I couldn't see his face, but I could tell he was eyeing his fallen weapon.

"You move one inch toward that shotgun and my next target will be the back of your skull," I said sternly.

He didn't acknowledge me. He kept his head turned, facing his gun.

"You've got two barrels staring you down, Harlan," I said. "Time to start talking."

He snapped his head at the mention of his last name.

"Cover me," I whispered to Billy.

I slid my Sig into its holster and climbed down. Once my feet hit the dirt, I slid it back out and aimed it straight at the killer.

"That's right," I said. "We know who you are. You and your serial killer brothers are going down."

He stared at me with intense, unflinching eyes. He was no longer wearing the bandanna. Grotesque burn scars covered most of his face, further fueling his evil persona.

I glanced down at the shotgun. I was confident that it wasn't his only weapon. Any moment, I expected him to grab a stashed handgun and try to take me out. If he did, he'd be dead before his hand clutched the grip.

"Who the fuck are you guys?" he spat, desperately struggling for his breath. "You're not the damn feds."

"It doesn't matter who we are," I said. "All that matters is that you make a choice. You can either die

151

right here in the dirt, or you can tell us where the others are."

I wasn't interested in taking down just one of the serial killers. I wouldn't be satisfied until everyone involved was either food for worms or locked up behind bars. They'd been murdering for far too long and it was time for all of them to get a taste of their own merciless medicine.

He eyed me like a caged animal. I could feel the anger surging from within him. It resonated from his dirt- and sweat-covered face in waves of hate-filled rage.

He turned away from me, then said, "Fuck you."

In the blink of an eye, he spun around and lunged toward me like a wild animal.

I fired off two rounds at the center of his body. Instead of hearing high-velocity lead striking soft flesh, I heard two loud and distinct tings. Metal on metal. Before I could shift my aim to his head, he was on me. It was more of a fall than a tackle as he collided into my body, sending us both tumbling to the dirt.

We rolled violently, cracking branches and thudding against trunks. He tried to wring my neck, but I kept him off me. His breath was foul, his stench ripe. Blood and saliva oozed from his mouth as we jerked to a stop. I glanced to my left and spotted the thick muddy pool of swamp water right beside the camp.

Being aware of your surroundings is crucial in any kind of fight. Even a less experienced fighter can take down a strong opponent if they use the terrain to their advantage. It can mean the difference between winning and losing. Between life and death.

He reached for something at the back of his belt.

A knife. I let him grab it, using the brief moment of relaxed tension to put space between us. With all my strength, I grabbed hold of his flabby flesh, twisted him as hard as I could, and hurled his body into the dark muck beside me.

He'd just grabbed hold of his knife and swung the tip toward me as he flew through the air. He stabbed the sharpened tip into nothing but mud as he oozed into the sinkhole, his body being sucked halfway into it as he landed.

I jumped to my feet and watched as he struggled to escape the mud. Every attempt only made his situation worse as he was sucked deeper and deeper.

His eyes grew wider than the horizon on the open ocean.

"Put me out of my misery," he demanded.

I caught my breath as I kept my Sig aimed at him. Billy had dropped down from the tree during the scuffle and was standing beside me. After a few seconds of no reply, the killer eyed us both with a devilish stare.

"Fine," he said angrily.

He ripped his knife from the mud and I almost pressed the trigger, thinking he was about to toss it in our direction. Instead, he rotated the blade around, aiming the tip straight at his chest, and pressed down forcefully. The knife sliced through his body, causing him to grunt and snarl as blood flowed out. He'd stabbed himself right through the heart.

Leaving the blade lodged in his body, he took a few more struggling breaths, then went motionless. Less than thirty seconds after he died, the sinkhole completely overtook his body and he vanished from view.

EIGHTEEN

Billy and I stood motionless, staring down at the bloody bog in front of us. I'd seen a lot of messed-up shit in my life, but watching a psychotic serial killer stab himself through his heart was a new one. It was beyond cringeworthy, and yet again I realized that I'd underestimated these guys. To say that they were a different breed was an understatement.

I swallowed, stepped back, and looked at Billy. He stared unblinking at the mud. There was a part of me that was relieved. We'd successfully tracked down and ended the life of a killer, a man with more innocent blood on his hands than we'd probably ever know. But with the killer dead, we no longer had anything to go on. He'd killed himself and been sucked into the mud, taking everything he knew with him. With the relief of his death came the unsettling truth that there were still two more brothers with pulses hiding out somewhere in the Glades.

I stepped over to the edge of the mud, bent over, and picked up the metal body armor that had been

154

ripped from the killer's body.

"Shit," I said, breaking what had felt like a ten-minute silence. "This thing's gotta way twenty pounds. This guy's been trekking through the swamp all day wearing this thing?"

At the center of the metal, I saw a cluster of small indents. I counted five in all, which meant that this guy had been shot at before. The armor was rugged, with rough edges and worn leather straps. It was homemade, that much was clear. Looked like it'd once been the door to an old fireplace, but it'd been cut and shaped to fit the guy's chest.

"Guess we can add blacksmith to their resumes as well," I said.

I moved back over toward the tent and snatched the shotgun from the dirt. The wooden stock was partially shattered just behind the trigger, and there were splatters of blood all over it. Looked like a Winchester pump-action, but it was hard to tell because they'd scratched and melted off all identifying markings. I popped open the chamber and saw a twelve-gauge shell ready to be fired and four in the tube.

"I've only ever seen one person die before," Billy said, speaking for the first time since the incident occurred.

I turned and saw him still standing as stoic as if his feet were stuck in dried concrete.

"But it wasn't like that," he continued, his words calm and clear. He sighed. "It was nothing like that."

I moved back over beside him, placing a hand on his shoulder.

"He was an evil man," I said. "It was gruesome and violent, but make no mistake, justice was served tonight."

Billy nodded.

"I know. But it's still a lot to take in, witnessing something like that."

He was right. I looked up through the canopy at a night sky full of stars. After a few more minutes, we headed back up into the tree and resumed our watches. Three gunshots had been fired, and in a place as open as the Glades, the sound would travel for miles. We couldn't risk another predator trying to sneak up on us in the night.

When it was Billy's turn to sleep, he kept his body up and his eyes wide open. He began talking in a hushed tone, telling me about how the Seminole tribe had come to live in the Everglades.

"We lived up north for many generations," he said. "Our tribe started out as bands of Creeks and other natives in Alabama and Georgia. They moved to Florida in the 1700s due to conflicts with Europeans. Soon, they became known as Seminoles or 'runaways.' They were a band of misfits, self-sustaining and living off the land. Over the years, their numbers increased as more natives joined the tribes and runaway slaves sought refuge among them. In the 1800s, tensions grew between the Seminoles and the white settlers. In 1817, future president Andrew Jackson launched the first of three wars against our tribe. Needless to say, the Indian Removal Act of 1830 didn't ease tensions. Our people fought being relocated, but most of us were wiped out. My fourth-generation grandfather, Osceola, led the tribe for many years."

"Wait a second," I said, shaking my head in bewilderment. "You're a descendant of Osceola?"

I didn't know a lot about history, but even I knew of the famous and influential Florida native, whose

156

army of ragtag warriors had fought back the US Army.

Billy nodded.

"After years of fighting and killing, American soldiers flew up the white flag of truce, indicating that they wanted to have peace talks with Osceola and a group of his men. But it was all a trap. It was later described as one of the most disgraceful acts in American military history, and it was. They captured Osceola along with his men. He was imprisoned and grew ill. He died just three months after being captured and was buried at Fort Moultrie in South Carolina."

I nodded.

"On Sullivan's Island," I said. "I visited the fort years ago."

Billy paused a moment and swallowed.

"The tribe fell apart after that," he continued. "Twenty years after Osceola's death, we'd been whittled down to just three hundred. The remaining Seminoles lived in hiding in the swamps. Today, our tribe has grown to a few thousand across six reservations in Florida."

I shifted my body to get a more comfortable position on the branches, then looked out over the dark landscape.

"These swamps are in my blood," he said. "Over eight generations have spent most of their lives here."

I nodded. I could see a powerful intensity burning in his eyes in the faint moonlight. Billy loved his land and the people who lived on it. This wasn't just about going after a few random serial killers. This was a personal mission for him.

We kept talking for over an hour. Having not spoken more than a few brief sentences all day, he'd clearly opened up after the incident. As an enlisted Navy sailor, I'd spent a lot of time standing watch in the middle of the night. Usually, you have a buddy with you to make sure you don't pass out, and it's always nice to have someone with interesting stories to tell. Makes the time pass faster.

I was interested in the history of his tribe, the rough and wild outcasts who'd lived in places just like where we were sleeping. He went on to tell me how he lived on the Big Cypress Reservation and that his family owned an RV resort there.

I was surprised to learn just how much Billy and I had in common. We were both thirty-two-years old, both only sons of career military men, his father having served nearly thirty years in the Coast Guard and my dad having retired as a master diver in the Navy. We were also both married to women that were way out of our league, though he already had three children.

"You guys want kids?" he asked.

I thought about it a moment. The truth was, Ange and I had talked about kids a few times since we'd gotten married. We both wanted them but wanted to enjoy a few more years of fewer responsibilities before taking on that chapter.

"Someday," I said.

With just a few hours left before sunrise and no sign of any additional visitors, we both decided to get a little sleep. I was a light sleeper and Billy told me that he was as well, so we figured that on the off chance anyone else did show up at our little camp, we'd wake up when they got close.

I woke up to the sound of my ringing sat phone. My blurry eyes opened. It was still dark, but as I sat up, I could see a faint distant glow to the east. I reached into my bag and grabbed my phone. Billy woke up as well and eyed me as I checked the screen and pressed the answer button. It was Ange.

"Good morning," I said.

"Nice to hear your voice," Ange replied. "I think I'm about to make your morning better."

"Better than being soaking wet in the middle of a swamp?" I said with a chuckle. "Good luck with that."

She laughed and told me that she might have something. I wasn't surprised. I'd grown to appreciate having a partner that was much smarter than I was. Ange often figured things out much quicker than I did.

"Oh? What'd you guys learn?"

"We watched the drone footage last night. After about the hundredth time through it, Jack spotted something."

"A boat?"

"No. Even better. A guy."

"How far upriver?"

"Nearly four miles," she replied. "Just before we turned around when the river breaks apart."

"A guy but no boat?" I asked suspiciously.

"Exactly. I think we may have a winner. You guys run into any trouble last night?"

"More like trouble ran into us," I said. "The killer snuck into our camp last night. Tried to tear us apart with shotgun pellets in our sleep. Too bad for him we decided to sleep up in a gumbo-limbo tree instead of in the tent."

"You kill him?"

"No. I gave him an ultimatum, then he jammed a knife through his heart."

She gasped. "Holy crap. I'm guessing he didn't

say anything, then?"

"Nothing useful. But now that you have a visual, we have something to go on. These killers live out here somewhere, and we're gonna find out where and pay them a little visit." I grabbed my GPS from my bag and added, "What are the coordinates for the place you spotted him?"

Ange read off the latitude and longitude, and I punched them into my GPS. After a few seconds, the screen pinpointed the location. It displayed a small island, and after checking it in relation to our current location, I saw that it was roughly three miles due east from us.

"We spotted the guy on the western side of the island," Ange said. "You see that muddy shoreline? He was standing right there. He quickly jumped beneath the canopy of trees when the drone flew overhead."

"This is good stuff, Ange. We'll head over that way and stake out the area. See if we can't track down any more killers."

Ange said something I couldn't hear, then said, "Alright. We'll head up the river. Make sure they don't get spooked and try and make a run for it." She paused a second, then added, "That stretch of water just southeast of the island could do nicely for landing the Cessna if we need to. It's short, but it could be done."

We agreed to keep each other posted, then I thanked her and we ended the call.

"We've got a bead on 'em," I said to Billy, who was eyeing me intently.

After a moment of no reaction and no answer, he tilted his head at me.

"What is it?" I said with a shrug.

160

"Nothing," he replied. "I've just never met a husband-and-wife pair like you two. You act as if this kind of situation is normal."

I couldn't help but smile.

"Chasing down bad guys?" I said. "Yeah, that's happened a few times." I looked out at the dense landscape surrounding us, then shouldered my backpack and motioned to the ground. After taking a few steps down, I held tight to a branch, straightened out my body, then let go. I bent my knees, absorbing the force as my boots hit the dirt. Looking up at Billy, I added, "Hunting down murdering rednecks in the Everglades? That's a new one."

"What line of work are you two in?" he asked, climbing down after me. "Pete told me a little about you, but not much. You were a SEAL, right?"

I nodded as he landed on the ground beside me. I stepped over to the tent and bent down. Unclipping one of the poles, I let one corner of the polyester sag down lifelessly, then stepped toward another corner.

"Come on," I said. "We've got another long day ahead of us. We can talk while we trailblaze."

NINETEEN

Buck Harlan stood in a narrow gap in the thick foliage covering a muddy shoreline. He held an old pair of binoculars up to his eyes and looked out over the flat, swampy landscape to the southwest. It was early. The sun hung just over the horizon to the east, casting a bright haze and warming the cool morning air.

After coming up empty yet again, he closed his eyes, lifted a dirty calloused hand, and squeezed his brow. He hadn't slept much. He'd spent most of the night standing right there, hoping to catch a glimpse of his brother. But no glimpse had ever come. In fact, no sign of human life had come aside from three gunshots in the middle of the night.

Signs of life, or signs of death?

Buck knew the answer to that question, but he didn't want to.

He heard labored footsteps coming down the trail behind him. He didn't have to turn around to know who it was. His brother Dale, similar in both size and stature, stopped just a few paces behind him. He moved with a bad limp which forced him to spend most of his time near their hideout.

"Still no sign of Jeb?" Dale asked, his voice rough and solemn.

Buck shook his head and spat a trail of tobacco juice onto the mud.

"What the shit, Buck? We gonna go after him now or what?"

Buck sneered. He jerked his head back and shot his younger brother a sinister look.

"You stupid twat. We can't go anywhere now thanks to you. You stood clear as day while that drone flew by. Just standing in the open like an idiot."

Dale paused a moment, then scratched his long messy beard.

"That stupid toy ain't gonna give us no trouble," he spat. "Besides, I ducked under the tree line before it flew overhead."

More like I tackled you, Buck thought. *And it wasn't a damn toy.*

Buck Harlan was a redneck who lived in the middle of nowhere, true, but he wasn't stupid. That thing had been high-tech. It flew fast, with a long range, and probably had a fancy camera on board. No, Buck knew his little brother was wrong. He knew that the "toy" would bring trouble.

"It's those same assholes we ran into in Hells Bay," Buck said. "I'm sure they killed Eli, too. We shoulda killed them when we had the chance."

They paused a moment, and Buck took another look through his binos.

"You getting riled up for nuttin'," Dale said. "We lived here forever and then some. Nobody finds us here. Every man who ever came close is dead and gone now. Besides, this is our home, Buck. We got the... oh shit, what's it called? The tactical advantage or something or other?"

His brother wasn't the brightest firefly, but he had somewhat of a point. Over the years, they'd rigged their little haven not only to be nearly imperceptible to onlookers, but also to be an attacker's nightmare. They'd accumulated a stockpile of various weaponry, including mines, grenades, and a handful of various types of guns and ammunition. Buck felt confident, but an uncomfortable itch crawled its way into his mind.

The man he'd tussled with in Hells Bay was different. He'd been a highly trained fighter, that much had been clear. But there was something else about the guy. Something in his eyes. He had strong motivation.

But what drove his motivation? And why had he come after them then?

Buck and his brothers had been killing off and on for years. The mysterious outsider with the plane had never shown up before. Finally, it clicked in his head.

That damn couple with the sailboat. Must've known 'em. Maybe even family.

He looked out over the water for what felt like the hundredth time already that morning. There was no sign of Jeb. He'd been gone for over twenty-four hours. They didn't have radios, so he knew his brother could still be out there. But he'd heard the gunshots the previous night. If his brother was alive, he'd be back already. It was time to face the truth.

Buck spat a wad of chewing tobacco and said, "Rig the island for full defense."

Dale looked at his brother with wide eyes and an open mouth.

164

"Rig the island for... ah shit, Buck. What the hell's the matter with you? Why aren't we goin' after Jeb?"

"Jeb's dead," Buck said. "And if we don't get ready, we'll be dead too."

Dale paused a moment. Suddenly, a surge of rage overcame him.

"We'll kill every last one of 'em," Dale said. "Solid oath to God I'll kill 'em all myself."

Buck nodded slowly. He felt the same anger coursing through his veins. He loved his brother and he vowed to avenge his death.

"Prepare the island," Buck said. "Get the gators in place. And don't feed Duke. I want him good and hungry when our guests arrive."

Turning around slowly, he stepped onto a narrow, zigzagging trail that cut toward the center of their island.

Looking back over his shoulder, he added, "They'll be here soon."

TWENTY

For three hours, we trudged through thick mangroves, sawgrass, and water. The Watson River broke off many times, forcing us to slog our way through deep channels, some of which reached our shoulders, making us hold our gear up over our heads as we kept a watchful eye out for gators and pythons.

We'd spotted over ten of the nonindigenous snakes since we'd started out the previous morning. The invasive species had been introduced to the area through a combination of storms destroying reptile zoos and negligent owners who didn't realize their little snakes would grow to be over ten feet long when their children had brought them home from the local pet store. If it were any other trip to the Glades, I'd kill each and every one I saw. But the last thing we wanted was to announce our location to the Harlan brothers. The remaining Harlan brothers, that was.

During the difficult morning trek, I'd told Billy a bit about me, starting with my years living in the Keys back when I was a kid in the '80s. He seemed

166

particularly interested in the circumstances that had brought me back to the island chain nearly twenty years after my dad had moved us away.

"I read about that Aztec treasure found near the Marquesas Keys," he said. "Didn't know you played a part in it, though."

"It was a group effort," I said. "And it was my friend Scott who initiated the whole thing."

"The senator," Billy said. "He's helped out the tribe a great deal. I hope you will give him my thanks when you see him again."

"Consider it done," I said.

"So, you've been living off the money from the treasure, then?"

"I got part of the finder's fee, which allowed me to buy a house in Key West," I said. "The money won't last forever, but we'll take life as it comes."

Billy fell silent for a moment, then said, "Pete said you knew the people killed last week."

"Yeah," I said. "The Shepherds. They were good friends of mine."

He nodded.

"I'm sorry for your loss. My uncle was killed here just last year. It's why Pete called me. He knew I was looking for these murderers."

I paused a moment, thinking over his words.

"Well, their killing days are coming to an end."

I glanced down at my GPS.

"Less than half a mile now," I said.

We reached a stretch of water roughly fifty feet wide.

"Too deep to wade," Billy said. "Looks like we're going swimming."

We stood for five minutes, examining the shore and making sure no gators were nearby before

167

climbing down a small bank to the murky water below. We reached the other side and hauled our dripping bodies up onto the opposite shore. Half an hour of trekking later, we reached the upper part of the Watson River. It cut westward, creating an L shape, and was much wider than any section we'd reached so far. After a few minutes of walking along the thick shoreline, we spotted the island we were looking for.

"You sure that's the spot?" Billy asked.

He was peering through his binoculars at a muddy shoreline a quarter of a mile away from us. It was a valid question. The island showed no sign of any human ever even stepping foot on it, let alone living there. It covered a decent amount of ground and looked to be roughly the size of a football field. The edges were covered in mangroves, the center with high-rising oak and cypress trees. It looked like any of the thousands of uncharted islands littering the Glades.

I stared down at the GPS one more time, just to be sure.

"Yeah," I said. "That's it alright." I reached into my backpack and added, "Keep eyes on it. I'm gonna call Ange with an update."

After Ange picked up, I told her that we'd reached the island. She replied, letting me know that they had the airboat up Watson and were idling about a mile south of us.

"You find anything?" she asked.

"There's no sign of life yet," I said. "We're gonna do a little recon, see what we can find. I think holding tight there for now is the best play. If we accidentally spook them, they might scatter like roaches."

"I've got my sniper locked and loaded," she replied confidently. "There's a quarter mile of straight unobstructed river north of us. If they try and come this way, I'll take them out before they even know we're here."

I nodded, told her to expect another call within the next hour or so, and hung up.

We looked over the southern part of the island for a few more minutes, then Billy suggested we walk around to the other side.

"I don't see anything here," he said. "Even the branches along the shore look undisturbed."

I agreed, and we moved slowly, concealing ourselves from view as best we could while hoping to catch a glimpse of movement on the island. If it wasn't their place, then I was confident that it was at least somewhere nearby.

"Holy hell," Billy said, freezing in his tracks.

He was staring at the western shore of the island, near the place where Ange said the drone had spotted someone. I blocked the sun from my eyes with a hand and focused on the shoreline. It wasn't a person, but rather a massive alligator sunbathing on the mud.

"That thing's gotta be over twelve feet long," Billy said. "Wait a second," he added, holding up a finger. "There's something off about it." He lifted his binos to get a better view. After a few seconds, he let out a breath and sighed.

"What is it?" I said.

I was about to grab my monocular out of my backpack when he said, "We found their place alright. That gator's got a metal collar around its neck. It's chained to the base of that cypress."

He handed me the binos and I focused in for a better look. He was right. The massive gator clearly had something around his neck. The chain was rusted but had a decent amount of slack.

"Quite the watchdog," I said.

Billy nodded, and as we continued, we realized that there was more than one. After an hour of recon, we counted three of the beasts in all, and that was just on the half of the island we were able to see without crossing the river. We also saw what looked like boot prints in the mud halfway up the western shore, though they were too far away to be certain that was what they were.

At 1000, after just over an hour of looking over the island, I gave Ange another call. It was time for us to meet up and formulate an attack plan.

After giving me their current coordinates, I said, "Just stay there. We'll come to you."

The last thing I wanted was for their motor to give us away. Plugging in their location, I saw that they were about three-quarters of a mile south of us.

"We've got a pole aboard," she said. "And this river moves about as fast as cold molasses. We'll head upriver to shorten the distance."

"Alright," I said. "Oh, you mind getting ahold of Mitch for me? I want to see if he has anything that can quietly and efficiently take down alligators."

Ange paused a moment.

"Something I should know about?" she said.

"These killers have got at least three of them chained up around the island."

"Great," she said, "guess that means we've for sure got the right place. I'll call him right away."

I thanked her, then trekked alongside Billy toward Watson. We moved low and out of sight from the island as best we could, keeping our eyes peeled for any movement and our ears alert for any unusual sounds. We soon reached the main section of the river, and within the hour, we saw the airboat moving briskly toward us, hugging the western shore.

We waved to get their attention, then hiked along the shore and stepped down the bank to the waterline. Ange was standing at the bow alongside Pete, while Jack sat on the bench seat, looking through a pair of binoculars. Just as we reached the water, Atticus vaulted from the airboat and ran through the mud toward us. By the time he reached me, he was covered in muck, but I didn't care. I dropped down to a knee and greeted my happy Lab, petting his thin yellow coat, and introduced him to Billy.

"Well, if it isn't the lost boys," Pete said. He stepped to the port gunwale and offered a hand. "You two look like a couple of bona fide swamp rats."

I let Billy climb aboard first. Pete was right. We were both covered in dirt, mud, sweat, and smelly clothes from being drenched and baked under the summer Florida sun.

"It sure helped having an expert by my side," I said. "Would have been a much longer twenty-four hours had he not been with me."

"I think you would have carried yourself just fine by yourself," Billy said.

I shrugged and climbed up onto the bow behind him with Atticus jumping up right on my heels. Ange stepped over, eyed me up and down, then grinned before we embraced in a big hug.

"You smell terrible," she said.

I cracked a smile. "Nice to see you too, Ange."

She laughed and kissed me by way of making amends.

She had her hair tied back and was wearing a Florida Marlins ball cap, jeans, and a thin long-

171

sleeved tee shirt. She smelled like she had about a gallon of bug spray covering her body. Her smooth, tanned skin was a delicacy among the mosquito community, so she always needed to use extra to fend them off.

After we let go of each other, I turned toward Jack. He started to rise from the bench seat, but I waved him off.

"I'm not crippled, bro," he jabbed.

I laughed, patted him on the shoulder, and asked how he was healing. By way of an answer, he lifted up his tee shirt and shifted his body so I could see the wound. The small gash to his side was covered with a white bandage.

"Martha at Flamingo stitched me up nicely," he said. "Didn't even need to see a doctor. Man, it's quite the badass experience to add to the old resume. 'You ever been shot by a forty-five?' Well, yeah, bro, I have and it barely fazed me. Might even impress a few girls now and then."

I laughed and we spent ten minutes catching up before getting down to business.

Ten minutes after arriving, we received a call from Mitch, letting us know that he was almost there. He'd tied off his airboat downriver and was paddling up on a kayak.

While Mitch made his way toward us, Billy and I told the others everything we knew, though it wasn't much. We told them the size of the island, its distance from shorelines, and about the alligator sentries.

"No sign of the two remaining brothers?" Jack said.

I shook my head.

"Only signs of life we could see were the chained-up gators," I said.

"The island was too overgrown to see more than just a short ways into it," Billy added.

We all paused a moment, thinking everything over.

"So let's go over the timeline," Pete said. "These brothers rob a bank, fake their deaths, then build a sanctuary in the Glades, far away from where anyone could find them, concealing it from outsiders by making sure it's surrounded by trees and whatnot."

"Then they start offing people," Jack said. "Seemingly at will."

"But not quite at will," Ange said. "Seems like they only killed people who came near their home."

"Ange is right," I said. "My guess is they've got some kind of partnership. Those drugs Ange found? I'm sure that wasn't all of it. I'd wager these guys have been selling coke for years, or more than likely just trading it for what things they needed. Fuel, necessities, food other than what you can find in the Glades, maybe."

"And whenever someone threatens their operation, they off them," Jack said.

I nodded. "That's the conclusion I've come to."

I spotted Mitch paddling toward us and raised a hand to silence our conversation. I wasn't sure that we could trust Mitch. After all, he'd been the one who'd vouched for Eli Hutt. For all we knew, Mitch was in on the entire operation. If that were the case, he could serve the other Harlan brothers intel from our circle. Hell, he could try and off us himself.

"Okay," I said, eyeing Pete and Billy with a serious gaze. "You both know Mitch and I need you to tell me if you trust him." I sighed and added, "Would you trust him with your life?"

"I've known him for five years," Pete said.

"He's a close family friend," Billy added. "We know him and his wife well."

"Neither of you answered my question," I said.

Billy and Pete both looked at each other, then nodded.

"Yes," Pete said. "I'd trust him with my life."

Billy said he would as well. I nodded. I'd gotten a good vibe from Mitch from the beginning, but the entire Eli Hutt incident had caused me to question whose side he was on.

"Alright," I said.

Mitch reached us a few minutes later. He tied his kayak to the bow of the airboat and climbed aboard. He was wearing his usual park ranger uniform and carried a black duffle bag in his right hand.

After a quick greeting, we continued with our discussion right where we'd left off.

"So, we barge onto the island and take them out?" Jack said. "I'm hoping there's some kind of plan here."

"I've got a few ideas," I said. "But I was counting on you guys to help me out with that."

"What are you thinking, Logan?" Pete asked.

"Well, for starters I'll swim onto the island quietly and take a look around. Then I'll give the all clear and call you guys in on the boat. My guess is they'll probably try and run for it, so you can cut off their escape."

"What about those gators?" Billy said.

Ange and I looked over at Mitch. He nodded, grabbed his duffle bag, and pulled out a black plastic hardcase.

"You'll put them to bed," he said to me confidently. Unclasping the hinges, he opened the case and pulled out a short narrow rifle and a clear case of darts.

"Tranquilizer gun?" Jack said.

Mitch nodded.

I'd seen many different types of tranquilizer guns before. The one he showed us was typically used by environmentalists looking to subdue animals in order to better track and care for them. It looked more like a paintball gun than a firearm, with a long narrow barrel connected to a simple body, scope, and stock. It had a small canister of CO_2 attached right in front of the trigger, which was used to propel the darts.

"It's a little worse for wear," he said. "I've had it for years now. But it's never let me down."

"You've put down gators with this thing?" Ange asked.

"Yep. The big ones sometimes take two shots." He opened the small case of darts and grabbed one. It was long and skinny, with a hypodermic needle on one end and a pink fuzzy tail on the other to stabilize it. "It's a special blend of immobilizing agents. I won't bore you with the chemistry, but it's designed especially for thick-skinned carnivores." He put the dart back in its case alongside the others and grabbed the rifle. "This gun has an effective range of fifty yards and is very accurate."

I thanked him for bringing it to us, letting him know that it would be nice to have during my infiltration of the island.

He paused a moment, thinking it over.

"So, you're not gonna call the police, then?" he asked.

Pete laughed. "Calling the police isn't exactly their style."

Mitch nodded. "I'm okay with that. The last thing I want is for these guys to get attention and

175

fame while the judicial system runs its long, winding course."

"I say we call them just as the engagement ends," I said. "It would be nice to give tourists a little peace of mind."

There was a short pause as we thought over everything.

"Plan seems pretty straight forward," Jack said.

"It is in theory," I said. "But I'm sure these guys will have more than one trick up their sleeves. They've got alligators chained to their beach, after all. Pete, you were right when you said not to underestimate these guys. They're a rough, skillful, and sadistic bunch. We need to be ready for the worst."

"Can't be harder than infiltrating an oil rig overrun by a private army, can it?" Jack said.

He was referring to an incident that had taken place earlier that year. A Zhao Petroleum drilling rig had been taken over by Carson Richmond and her Darkwater thugs. Thankfully, she'd met a quick and fiery end when her helicopter had blown to pieces while she was trying to make an escape.

"Wait," Mitch said, "you were involved in that—"

"Don't listen to Jack," I said, shooting him a look. "He speaks without thinking sometimes."

"Say, you could always parachute in like you did on the rig," Jack continued, seemingly oblivious to the fact that our participation in the events on the oil rig had been kept secret.

"The canopy is too thick to drop in," I said. "I'd get tangled and hang high up. A sitting duck."

I thought about my idea of swimming to the island and knew that it would be anything but easy.

First, the water was so murky that it would be difficult to see my hand in front of my face. Next, I didn't know how deep it was. We were literally in uncharted territory. The upper portions of the Watson were barely marked on the charts we had, and no depths were given. Then there were also the gators to worry about.

We talked for a few more hours while eating sandwiches and drinking coconut water under the shade of the small pop-up canopy. We took intermittent glances both up and downriver and around the surrounding prairie swamps to ensure that no one was trying to sneak up on us.

"I like your plan, but I'm making a few minor changes," Ange said. "For starters, I'm coming with you. And second, we're gonna take a more stealthy approach."

She opened a large compartment, reached inside, and pulled up two Draeger rebreathers.

"You brought the rebreathers?" I said with a smile.

"Of course I did. I know how much you love sneaking up on bad guys."

TWENTY-ONE

Dark clouds swept across the sky as Ange and I gathered up our gear. It was 1300 by the time we hopped onto the shore and headed across a long stretch of swampy prairies toward the island. Thunder roared far in the distance. The wind picked up, causing small whitecaps to form even on the narrow river.

Half an hour later, we reached the shoreline we'd chosen to enter from. A tiny curve in the water and a cluster of thick cypress trees blocked the island from view. But we knew where it was. We'd spent an hour on the boat going over our route. In order to minimize the risk of being seen, we'd need to navigate our way nearly a quarter of a mile through unknown depths and murky water.

As we donned our gear, we felt the first raindrops. Seconds later, we were being drenched as the heavens opened up, pelting us with thick sheets of water. Thankfully we both zipped up our drysuits just in time. I also had all of my gear, including the hardcase with the tranquilizer gun, stowed in my waterproof bag. The only thing I'd allow to get wet was my Sig, which I strapped to my leg outside my drysuit. The SEALs handgun of choice for years was designed to be fired even underwater if necessary. In all the years I'd shot the handgun, the thousands of rounds I've put through it, I've never had a misfire. Rain or shine, it's as reliable as a weapon can get.

Once we had our drysuits on it was time to set up and don the rebreathers. The beauty of rebreathers is that they're a closed-loop system, so instead of exhalations bubbling up to the surface, gases breathed out are scrubbed, mixed, and returned to be used as breathable air. It makes the advanced diving apparatus the optimal choice when stealth is a factor. Rebreathers also make buoyancy control in the water much easier, since you don't constantly bob up and down with each breath cycle. The only downside is they're far more expensive and complex than scuba gear, requiring a high level of knowledge to operate. I've used them for years, and I still occasionally forget to do something in the start-up process.

It took a few minutes, but once we were done, we strapped them onto each other's backs. Once the diving apparatuses were ready, we set up our dive computers. The thunder grew louder and mixed with occasional strikes of lightning. Rains continued to slam against us, holding nothing back as the wind pounded the drops against our bodies and gear.

I smiled as I dummy-checked all of Ange's hoses, straps, and gauges. We made brief eye contact, and her expression quickly shifted from serious to confused.

"What could possibly make you so cheery at a time like this?" she said, her Swedish accent stronger than usual.

"I was just thinking about that island in Tahiti," I said. "It would sure be nice to be there right now."

"Nah," Ange said sarcastically. "I'd much prefer to be hanging out in a swamp, diving into water with zero viz while heavy rain beats down on me and massive alligators lurk nearby. That sounds much more exciting."

I gave a slight laugh.

"You forgot the serial killers. Relaxing with nothing to do on that island sure looks good. Maybe we'll head back there. Kick back in a place with a little less trouble."

Ange smiled and shook her head.

"Don't kid yourself, Dodge. A few months of that lifestyle and you'd be antsy, itching for your piece of some kind of action."

She knew me better than anyone else. I'd run into trouble many times in my life. Sometimes it was the product of my looking for it; other times it had fallen in my lap. But one way or another, I'd found myself in dangerous situations time and time again. That was just the way my life had been. I enjoyed it, though. The rush of the chase, the feeling of adrenaline during a fight, and the sense of purpose when you stop evil in its tracks. It'll get me killed one day if I don't keep it in check. Maybe one day it'll fade away and I'll be... content.

Ange waded into the water, her boots sinking into the mud with each step. I slid my mask over my face and moved in right beside her.

It won't be today. Today we'll look danger in the eye and show anything but fear.

We both donned our fins when the muddy water reached our chest. I glanced at my dive computer, which had a built-in compass, to make sure we were oriented in the right direction. We nodded to each other, both took one more look at the world above, then dropped down into murky darkness.

Moving side by side, we kicked forward and flattened out our bodies. The soft bottom of the river was so close I could stretch out my hand and touch it. Reaching across my body, I pressed a button on my dive computer to illuminate the screen. We were in six feet of water, shallow by diving standards but plenty deep enough to keep ourselves hidden. Staying in line with each other, we took off across the river, finning with smooth strokes.

Having a plan is an essential part of any dive, recreational or otherwise. This is especially true when diving in water with zero visibility where the depths are unknown. River diving, regardless of how slow-moving the water is, also presents a number of potential hazards, including shifting, unknown obstacles. It was far from an ideal, safe dive, so we'd prepared for it earlier on the boat as best we could before heading out.

The key to diving when you can't see anything is being aware of how far you travel with every kick cycle. Different gear configurations yield different results due to weight distribution and drag. Ange and I both knew the approximate distance we traveled with that gear underwater with each cycle. Mine was about twelve feet and hers was about eight, so I kicked softer and she kicked harder so we could stay in line with each other. We had roughly thirteen hundred feet of distance between us and the island, so that meant approximately one hundred and thirty kick cycles. It wouldn't be exact, but it would give us a pretty good idea of where we were in relation to the island at all times.

We finned to a rhythm, occasionally adjusting our course to stay in line. The cooler water near the bottom was a welcome relief to the hot, humid air above. I did my best not to think about what deadly creatures could be lurking nearby and tried to focus on each kick and prepare for what I'd do once we reached our destination. We ran into a few branches and navigated around two shallow banks, but for the most part, the dive went smoother than I'd expected. Ten minutes after dropping beneath the water, I counted the final kick cycle. We touched the bottom of a muddy shoreline just moments later.

I removed my fins, clipped them onto my waist, and snatched my Sig from its holster. Slowly and quietly, we planted our boots and rose up out of the water. Our masks broke the surface at the same time as the barrels of our weapons did. Surprisingly, the rain still splashed down around us, though it was clearly dying down. We stayed still for a few seconds, just barely peeking over the dirty surface while our eyes scanned the mud-lined bank. It was clear of all movement aside from the breeze swaying branches and the tree canopy overhead. There was no sign of life aside from two massive gators sprawled out on the shore. One was lying less than fifty feet in front of us. The other was down the shore a ways.

I tilted my head, glanced over at Ange, then gave a slight nod of my head. We switched off our rebreathers, then slowly and silently moved out of the water. We rose up onto a patch of grass, and I quickly snatched the hardcase from my waterproof bag. Before removing any of my gear, I opened the case, grabbed the already-loaded tranquilizer gun, and took aim. The closest gator was eyeing us suspiciously.

We were just one wrong move away from making the territorial carnivore charge at us, so I wanted to subdue it first thing.

Ange covered my six as I pulled the trigger. A nearly silent and instantaneous hiss of CO_2 launched the dart, sending it flying through the air and stabbing into the center of the gator's body. The needle punctured deep through the gator's thick skin, causing it to snap open its jaw and jerk for a few seconds before becoming lifeless in the mud.

With the closest threat neutralized, we quickly unclipped and slid out of our gear. Once unzipped, the drysuits came off easy, and in less than a minute we were ready to go. We hid everything we wouldn't need under a tangle of mangroves, then turned to head down the shore toward the other gator. We couldn't tell exactly how long its chain leash was but reasoned that there was a good chance it could reach us if we didn't put it to bed.

I loaded another dart in the gun, and before we'd taken two steps down the shoreline, Ange nudged me.

"Remember what Mitch said." She glanced back at the motionless gator. "Two for the big ones. I'd say these monsters fit the bill."

I nodded, turned around, and put another dart in the first gator.

We kept a sharp eye out for the Harlan brothers as we turned and closed in on the second gator. When we were well within range, I reloaded another dart and sent it flying. The massive gator reacted much like the first had, with a few snarls and quick movements before going still.

But as I reloaded another dart, it lifted its head and stared straight at us.

"Logan," Ange said, watching the creature

intently.

Suddenly, its jaw snapped open and it took off down the shore, sprinting right for us. I'd read that alligators could sprint in short bursts in excess of thirty-five miles per hour. Seeing the massive creature take off sent a chill down my spine as I quickly raised the gun to give it a much-needed second dose of knockout juice.

I pulled the trigger and heard a quiet click, but nothing happened. The gun had jammed.

So much for never disappointing.

I dropped the gun and quickly snatched my Sig. I watched and listened as the angry gator made a beeline straight for us. The rusted chain holding him in place rattled, went taut, then snapped at a weak link.

You've gotta be kidding me.

I kept my Sig raised and aimed it straight at the fast-moving gator, though I knew that a barrage of 9mm rounds wouldn't do anything aside from pissing it off even more and alerting anyone on the island to our presence. It closed the gap in a matter of seconds and snapped open its jaw, revealing rows of large jagged teeth. Just as it was about to try and turn me into a snack, Ange lunged from the corner of my eye and slammed the tip of her knife into the top of its head.

In an instant, the angry carnivore's eyes shot up into its skull, and it collapsed limply on the mud. Ange withdrew her knife and the gator rolled lifelessly into the water. I kept my Sig aimed at it for a few seconds just to make sure. But it was dead, killed instantly by the sharp tip of Ange's dive knife.

We both fell silent and looked around, making sure no one had heard our little scuffle. Ange washed the blood from her knife in the water, slid it back into its sheath, and grabbed her Glock.

After a few moments, I whispered, "That was a money shot."

Killing a large gator isn't easy. Shooting it in the tail or in the head won't do anything. Shooting its underbelly might kill it eventually, but won't help you short-term. But there's one surefire way to take down a gator, and it's called the kill spot. Roughly the size of a quarter, the kill spot is located just behind a gator's skull. Shoot or stab at this spot, at just the right angle, and you can reach their small brains, killing them instantly. But it isn't easy, especially when the gator's running full speed.

I patted her on the shoulder, thanked her for saving me.

"And to think you were planning on coming alone," she said.

We moved up the bank and into the dense jungle. After a few steps, we heard voices coming from the center of the island. They were male. Low, rough baritones. Just like the guy I'd shot and thrown into a sinkhole the previous night. It was the other Harlan brothers, and if they were talking normally, it meant that they didn't know we were there.

I paused a moment, eyeing the ground. Ange pushed aside a dense branch and took one step ahead of me. Spotting something strange, I grabbed the back of her right arm and pulled her back to me. She eyed me like I was crazy, then looked down at the ground as well. There was a thin, nearly impossible to see fishing line strung out just above the sand and dirt. Following the line, I saw that one end was tied off to a tree trunk and the other to a metal device covered with leaves. An explosive of some kind.

Ange gasped. "I guess now we're even."

TWENTY-TWO

"Maybe you should go first," Ange said, taking a step back.

Her gaze was still glued to the booby trap in front of us.

"What happened to ladies first?" I said with a smile.

I dropped down to one knee and lowered my head under the brush line for a better look.

"Get with the times," she said jokingly. "That's sexist talk these days."

I shook my head, cracked a little smile. Opening doors for women and letting them go first was a part of me that would never change, regardless of the times. But if she insisted, I'd take the lead given the circumstances.

I leaned forward carefully, examining the booby trap. It looked like a typical tripwire mechanism. The taut fishing line most likely led to some form of fragmentation or bouncing mine. I'd encountered and been trained on how to disarm a tripwire explosive.

Given the highly advanced and sophisticated nature of the US military, we'd oftentimes resorted to using Silly String to spot tripwires during missions in the forested regions of Iraq. The lightweight strings would settle on the ground in areas with no wire and would rest on taut wires without being heavy enough to trigger the explosive.

Since I didn't have the proper tools to disarm it and we wanted to move fast, we opted for the "carefully stepping over the line" method.

"I've never been more thankful for your good eyes," Ange said after we carefully traversed it.

We moved slowly, keeping a sharp eye out for any more traps. As I'd expected, these guys had a few tricks up their sleeves. They weren't inept, that much was clear. Murdering criminals, yes, but not dumb. That was how they'd been so successful all these years, how they'd managed to kill and sell drugs without being caught.

I raised a hand and we both froze as voices emanated from the center of the island once more. They were louder, though not loud enough to understand. We were getting closer.

"Would you look at that?" Ange whispered. She pointed to our left at what looked like a small footpath that cut right through the dense foliage. "Not exactly a yellow brick road, but it'll work."

I smiled and we both carefully stepped over to it. Since we were close to the center of the island and now had an easy route to follow, I grabbed my sat phone and called Jack.

"They're here," I said quietly. "Time to spook these pests." I paused a moment, then added, "Steer clear of the land for now. It's rigged with traps."

"Roger that," Jack said. "T-minus one minute to

188

game time."

The second I hung up, I started the stopwatch on my dive watch. Bent low and hunched out of sight, we closed in. The path was narrow and zigzagged a few times, but we didn't run into any more traps. The thick tangles of brush gave way at the center of the island, revealing a clearing. We dropped down near the base of the tree and leaned around for a better look.

A few hundred feet from us, we could see a pair of long, skinny tin roofs that were covered in overgrown vines. In the distance, I saw a large covered dome with a door. We'd reached their hideout, but the voices had died off, so there was no way of knowing where they were.

I glanced down at my dive watch. Just as the counting numbers hit sixty, I heard the sound of an engine start up in the distance. It grew louder and louder within seconds as the airboat flew toward the island from the east. The sounds of voices returned. They were slightly muffled, but we could make out what they were saying.

"Get the fuck up there and take them out!" a loud, powerful voice yelled.

Ange and I were kneeling beside each other, our handguns scanning over the hideout. We'd heard them but couldn't see them. It was like they were ghosts.

What the hell is going on?

"You see an—" Ange said, then cut herself off in an instant.

A tall, round-bellied man wearing a cutoff camo shirt and torn-up muddy jeans suddenly appeared out of nowhere. He was clearly one of the brothers, the one I hadn't seen yet. Unlike his bald-headed kin, he had short dark hair with an ugly receding hairline and a long scraggly beard. He wore a serious expression on his face and gave a loud grunt as he moved toward something out of view. He looked like he had a knee injury due to the way he labored and struggled to run. In his hands, he gripped what looked like a Thompson submachine gun.

"Shit!" Ange said.

We both locked on to him with our pistols. But as quickly as he'd appeared, he vanished behind a row of branches and bushes. We couldn't see where he'd gone, but his intentions were clear. He was planning to take down our backup on the approaching airboat.

"Come on!" I said.

Before the words left my lips, we were both sprinting in a low crouch along the edge of the camp. We kept our eyes forward, taking intermittent glances just in case the other brother decided to make a move on us. By the time we got a clear view of the long-bearded guy, he was halfway up the trunk of a large cypress tree, using blocks of wood they'd nailed in place to create a ladder.

He reached a small platform thirty feet in the air, situated where two branches intersected side by side into the trunk. It was like a duck blind, covered with green growth in all places aside from a wide window that had a clear view of the river.

The sound of the airboat's engine and propeller were getting louder with every second. They were closing in on the island. We took cover behind a large stump and watched as the big guy lifted his Tommy gun, the tip of the barrel visible through the opening.

The jig was up. It was time for us to make our presence known.

Before he had the gun butt against his shoulder,

Ange and I both opened fire. We each sent a single round splintering through the side of the platform. The brother groaned, dropped the gun, and lost his balance. The force from the rounds forced his body sideways. He toppled over the side, letting out a primal yell as he went into a free fall. His big pudgy frame spun twice before slamming hard into the ground.

We couldn't see his body after the fall. He was hidden from our view, having landed and tumbled near the northwest corner of the island. It didn't matter. He was no longer a concern of mine. Two rounds center mass and an awkward thirty-foot fall didn't bode well for him.

We quickly turned our attention back toward the center of their hideout. We expected the third and final brother to appear with a surge of vengeance that would give Captain Ahab chills. Instead, we heard the loud and unmistakable sound of a barking dog.

A large German Shepherd appeared near the center of the camp. It barked violently, bared its teeth, and jumped up and down, trying to take off in our direction. But he couldn't—he was being held back.

Right behind the dog, the third brother appeared. It was the biggest brother, the one I'd wrestled two days earlier in Hells Bay. He looked exactly the same except for a black bandanna with a skull that was tied over his bald head. His face was still painted dark, his clothes tattered and dirty as hell. He had a revolver in his left hand and a baseball-sized object in his right hand.

Just as his upper body appeared, he reared the object back and hurled it straight toward us. It took my mind a fraction of a second to process what I was seeing.

A grenade.

There was no time to speak. No time to contemplate what we should do.

I spun around, wrapped my right arm around Ange, and forced us over the large stump behind us with all my strength. In a slow-motion blur, we flew through the air and crashed into a thick tangle of branches on the other side. As soon as we hit the ground, I rolled Ange over so that she was against the corner of the stump, then covered her with my body. I was gambling with my life. I'd only seen the grenade's trajectory for an instant before turning around. If I'd misjudged its speed and it flew over the edge of the stump, I was dead.

As soon as I shielded Ange with my body, the grenade exploded. A loud and powerful boom rattled the air and shook the ground. My body was tense and pressed hard against Ange's. I'd prepared for pain, expecting shards of sharp shrapnel to stab into my body. But none came.

I let out a breath. My heart was pounding, booming inside my chest. I pushed myself away from Ange and looked her over briefly. She tilted her head, her eyes wide as she made eye contact with me.

There was no time to ask how she was, no time to discuss the fact that we'd both just been fractions of a second from meeting a painful end.

As the explosion subsided, the loud intense barking again filled the air. It was louder. I could hear the dog's snarling and its paws landing on the dirt as it sprinted toward us. I peeked over the stump, Sig in hand, ready to take it out. I loved dogs and hated the idea of hurting one, but I knew that this badly trained pooch would bite and claw us to shreds if given the chance.

Just as I popped up into view and spotted the dog hightailing it right for us, gunfire erupted behind it. I caught a quick glance of the third brother. He was barely in view, aiming and firing his rifle in our direction. I dropped back down as a succession of bullets struck the other side of the stump. He was covering his dog's deadly approach.

Ange and I scrambled into a crouching position. She rolled sideways, popped up, and fired two rounds at the brother. He stopped firing momentarily, and a second later, the German Shepherd hurled itself over the stump and into my field of vision.

It dove right at me, its heavy frame slamming into mine, tackling me and pinning me against the ground. The beast of a dog growled and drove its teeth-riddled mouth toward me. It took everything I had to keep space between us. This wasn't an ordinary attack dog. It had the size, the aggression, and the killer look in its eyes of a starving wolf.

Digging my hands into its neck and body, I tried to force it off me but ended up causing both our bodies to roll, cracking small branches beneath us. My backpack flew from my body. The straps holding the hardcase in place loosened enough for it to break free. It tumbled beside me, the force causing the case to break open like a steamed clam.

I wrapped my hands around the ravenous canine's neck, using all my strength to keep it from biting the hell out of me. Drool dripped from its sharp teeth. I could feel the intensity of its anger resonating from its body.

With my back jammed against the ground, I was unable to grab my new hunting knife. Glancing briefly to my right, I saw the open hardcase and the tranquilizer gun resting inside of it. The pink fuzzy

193

part of the dart that hadn't been fired was still barely sticking out of the chamber. Keeping my left hand wrapped around the dog's neck, I reached as far as I could with my right. The animal forced itself into me, digging its teeth into my shoulder and biting down hard. I yelled as the sharp pain surged. My right hand struggled blindly, gripping the dart, and I forced it free from the gun.

The dog continued to bark maniacally. It clawed one of its paws across the side of my chest, digging the sharp edges deep through my skin. The pain was intense, but I did my best to ignore it as I gripped the dart and stabbed the needle into the dog's side. The plunger slid all the way forward, injecting the sedating liquid. It took effect almost instantly, causing the dog's growling to quiet and its body to go limp.

I shoved the heavy unconscious pooch off me and saw Ange crouched beside the stump. She was holding her Glock in one hand, her dive knife in the other. Clearly, she'd been just about to stab the dog when I'd put it to sleep. The brutal scuffle had lasted just a few quick seconds, but it had felt like much longer.

I rose up, grabbed my Sig, and moved beside her.

"Are you okay?" she said, eyeing my chest and shoulder.

The dog had clawed my shirt to pieces, and blood oozed out from both wounds.

I nodded.

"Minor scratches."

Bullets fired off yet again, interrupting us as they hammered into the other side of the wood. The truth was that my wounds were anything but minor. They hurt like hell, and the only reason I wasn't screaming in pain was because of the adrenaline coursing through my veins.

Ange and I lowered our bodies even more, and I inched closer to her.

"I'll flank him," I said.

She nodded, waited for our attacker to stop shooting, then popped up and fired off a few rounds to cover me. I sprang to my feet and took off across the hideout. I had my Sig gripped with both hands and my eyes locked on to the place where I'd seen the third brother moments earlier. My heart continued to pound, but I kept the weapon stable. The moment he appeared, he'd be dead. I'd put a round through his skull before he could blink.

My mind focused and my breathing steady, I moved in. The camp was surprisingly barren. A few camouflage tarps concealed tin roofs covering large plastic barrels and metal cooking utensils. Gas tanks, a grill, what looked like a water-collection system of some kind with a cistern. But there was no sign of the remaining brother.

Up ahead, beside a large barrel, there was a round sheet of metal on the ground. It was covered in dirt and was resting at an odd angle. When I stepped closer, I realized what it was. A hatch.

I looked around, then dropped down and wrapped my fingers around the edges. I lifted it up and threw it aside, revealing a wide hole in the ground. Leaning over, I saw a metal-rung ladder leading down the side of a metal tube. I could see light flickering and hear the shuffling of feet coming from the bottom roughly ten feet below.

How in the hell did these guys build this thing?

I looked at the hole in awe for a few seconds, then turned back to look at Ange, who was eyeing me questioningly from behind the shot-up stump.

With my right hand clutching my Sig, I waved her over with my left. She stood up, slid over the log, and ran over to me while keeping her head on a swivel. Before she'd reached me, I dropped down and grabbed hold of the first rung. Sliding my hands across to the metal bars that ran the vertical length of the ladder, I took in a deep breath. My chest and shoulder were both bleeding and hurt like hell. But I'd chased these assholes through the Glades, and I wasn't about to let a few cuts stop me from finishing the job.

Here we go.

I slid my boots to the outer bars and let my body slide down quickly as I maintained control using pressure from my extremities. I reached the bottom in seconds. The soles of my boots made contact with a concrete floor, and I bent my knees to absorb the shock, landing as quietly as possible.

Gripping my Sig with both hands, I quickly scanned the small, rustic room. It was a dirty, worn-down living space. A few metal bunk beds with stained mattresses and scattered ragged blankets. An old table and chairs. Shelves filled with stacked canned foods, dehydrated meals, and dried jerky meat. The floor was covered in dirt. The place looked about how the brothers did. Dirty and smelly and in dire need of a good cleaning.

Near the back, I spotted a closed wooden door. There were muddy boot prints on the ground leading under it.

My Sig at the ready, I stepped toward the door and tried the handle. It was locked. I stayed silent for a few seconds, listening for any sign of life on the other side. These guys had rigged their island with

196

traps and vicious animals. I did my best to prepare for whatever game this last asshole was playing.

I was in pain and had lost a decent amount of blood. But I manned up, leaned back, and slammed my right heel as hard as I could into the door. It shattered from its frame, fell forward, and landed on the floor.

I waited for a cloud of dust to clear, then stepped through. The doorway led to an even smaller room. There were metal shelves with stacks of black duffle bags on both sides. Straight across from me, I saw another ladder. Stepping across the room, I looked up and saw bright light bleeding down from overhead. It was smaller than the main tunnel, but still plenty wide enough for even the big Harlan boys to crawl through.

I heard a sound back in the main room. Looking back, I saw Ange land on the floor and spin around. She walked through the doorway and examined the small room with stacked plastic packages.

"Looks like we found the mother lode," Ange said.

I nodded, then turned to look at the small escape ladder.

Suddenly, Ange and I froze as we heard the sound of a large outboard engine start up.

It wasn't our backup. Their engine was already running—we could hear it humming in the distance near the other side of the island. This was one of the Harlan brothers' airboats. He'd led us down here so he could run up and try and make an escape.

"That coward's trying to make a run for it!" I said, gritting my teeth as I slid my Sig into its holster and took on the ladder as fast as I could.

I quickly reached the top. Grabbing my Sig, I moved toward the northern shoreline and the sound of the newly started engine. I heard the whoosh of a giant fan. The sound was coming from the camouflage-painted structure I'd originally thought was their house. I sprinted across the camp and shouldered my way inside.

It was a small rustic boathouse. Half of it was wide open, revealing a muddy bank covered in mangroves. Vines and branches hung down from all sides. From the outside looking in, it looked like ordinary untamed shoreline. The brothers had clearly used it to quickly hide their boats for years.

Just as I entered, the final brother's airboat took off across the water, picking up speed as it headed directly away from me.

It was like déjà vu with this guy. I aimed my Sig and pulled the trigger, firing round after round toward him and his rapidly escaping boat. The lead struck, shooting up sparks but not slowing the fan.

I heard footsteps behind me. When the slide of my Sig locked back, indicating that the magazine was spent, I glanced over my shoulder and saw Ange moving toward me.

"The sat phone," she demanded, holding out her hand.

"It's in my backpack," I said, motioning toward the other side of the hideout.

Ange shook her head. "Ah, hell with it."

She strode through the mud right up to the shoreline. While the killer's boat was growing fainter, ours was growing louder. We could hear it motoring toward us, rounding the northwestern part of the island.

Lifting her right thumb and index finger up to her mouth, she let out a loud squeaky whistle. Billy motored the airboat into view just a few hundred feet offshore. Jack and Pete were standing at the bow, weapons at the ready.

Ange and I both pointed toward the final brother, who was motoring off to the west.

Billy looked from us to the escaping boat and nodded.

"We'll get him!" Pete shouted at the top of his lungs.

Billy hit the throttles, giving it everything she had and rocketing their airboat into their quarry's wake.

Ange and I stood side by side for a few seconds, trying to think of a way to help with the chase.

Now might be a good time to get the authorities involved, I thought. *But we'll need more than a strong whistle to do it.*

I was just about to turn around and go after my backpack when I heard shuffling in the dense foliage beside us.

Is it another gator? Or maybe their not-so-friendly pooch has woken up from his nap?

Ange and I both aimed our weapons at the unknown sound. A moment later, I realized that neither of my guesses were right.

"Buck!" the brother we'd shot yelled at the top of his lungs as he stepped into view along the shore. He moved with slow, jerky steps. He had his hands pressed to his side, trying to stop the gushes of blood that were flowing out and dripping onto the mud at his feet. "No! How dare you leave me. No! You son of a bitch, Buck!"

His yells were loud and filled with rage. His body shook as he stopped and let out a powerful, barbaric cry.

His brother's airboat was almost out of sight. If

he'd heard the dying screams of desperation behind him, he didn't show it.

The angry bleeding brother suddenly jerked his head sideways, realizing that Ange and I were standing there for the first time. We were only about twenty feet away from him and both had our weapons aimed straight at him. I'd reloaded my Sig and now had fifteen fresh 9mm rounds. Two apparently hadn't done the trick with this guy, not quickly enough anyway.

His face contorted as his bulging eyes stared daggers at us. Veins stuck out of his dirty forehead. His teeth chattered like he was freezing to death.

He took a slow, labored step toward us.

"You," he said, channeling all of his anger toward me. "You fucker. You did all of this."

He reached for a knife sheathed to his belt. I was about to pull the trigger and put him out of his misery when Ange raised a hand to stop me.

"He's not worth the ammo," she said. "I've got him."

She stepped toward the guy, and before he could remove his weapon, she hit him with a powerful side kick. Ange's heel drove hard into his belly, causing his body to fly backward. He grunted loudly and started to scream but was silenced as he splashed into the murky water.

One of the nearby gators saw and was attracted to the commotion of the struggle. It ran into the water just down the shoreline, chain in tow. An injured animal attracts a predator like a magnet. It's something innate, something primal deep within its psyche.

The dying brother struggled just to lift his head up out of the water. He managed to get two quick gulps of air before the gator closed in on him. It was over quickly. A powerful snapping of jaws. A final scream of agony. And then the gator pulled him under.

Blood and air bubbles floated up to the surface. After a few seconds, the water went still.

I directed my gaze back up toward the western horizon, watching as our airboat disappeared in the distance.

TWENTY-THREE

Billy kept his eyes forward, his right hand gripping the airboat's rudder stick hard and his foot pressed to the accelerator. The engine groaned and the propeller roared at his back, shooting them across the water. He took off after the last surviving brother with reckless abandon, weaving in and out of sharp turns and skidding over shallows.

He knew the river as well as anyone. Knew that it was about to completely die off, to break apart into narrow strips that were too small to navigate an airboat through.

He'll be trapped soon, he thought. *He'll be trapped and we'll finish this.*

Pete and Jack were crouched down in the bow. They kept low to avoid the gusts of strong wind slapping against their bodies and held on tight to prevent being launched out into the water with every turn. As their boat closed in on their enemy, they fired off a few rounds, trying to take the killer down and put an end to the chase.

With the river dying off ahead of them, Buck cut a hard left into a shallow channel that was just wide enough for his boat to fit through. Billy followed, flying into the wake without hesitation. Their boat was bigger, however, and it scraped against the mangroves on either side. Overhanging branches slapped against their bodies. Logs and debris filled the channel, forcing him to slow down as the hull bounced and rattled every few seconds.

Billy gazed up ahead. They were within a hundred yards of their enemy, and the channel was about to get even narrower.

"Be ready!" Billy shouted over the ear-rattling sounds of the airboat. "We're about to reach the end of the line!"

Billy eased back to thirty knots. To his astonishment, Buck maintained his daredevil pace.

Is this guy about to try and off himself?

The question lingered in his mind for only a second before he saw something up ahead that caused his eyes to grow wide and his mouth to drop open. He watched as Buck grabbed what looked like a machete, jumped out of his seat, and leaned over the port side of his airboat. With his boat continuing to rocket forward, he slashed the machete at the water like a madman.

Just as Billy was about to yell out that he'd gone crazy, a large object splashed out of the water in front of them, just behind their quarry's stern. It took Billy's eyes a moment to focus, and he realized that it was a metal barrier of some kind. He only had a moment to react. At their speed, they'd crash into the obstruction in seconds.

He lifted his foot off the throttle. Knowing that there was only one way to slow them down in time, he jerked the rudder stick back, sending the airboat into a fast spin. It rotated three full times before skidding to a stop as it screeched against the metal grill that rose up out of the water.

They watched as Buck climbed back into the control seat, looked back over his shoulder, then turned sharply out of view. The metal bars of the barricade were held strongly in place. Pete and Jack both leaned over to try and push it down or out of the way, but it was no use.

Billy killed the airboat's engine. They listened as the brother's airboat grew fainter and fainter.

"You've got to be kidding me, man," Jack said. "What the hell is it with these guys?"

"He's a pesky slimy vermin," Pete said, shaking his head. He stepped toward the center of the boat, grabbing the radio from his bag. "We need to call in reinforcements. He's on the run. Desperate. We can still get him."

TWENTY-FOUR

Buck Harlan could feel his pursuers breathing down his neck. They were closing in. Three guys, looked like. All of them armed, no doubt. If they caught up to him, he'd be done for.

He stared anxiously up ahead at a river that was growing narrower and narrower by the second.

Almost there. Less than a quarter mile now.

His heart pounded and he gritted his teeth. He kept his mind focused on the terrain that he knew like the back of his own hand. He couldn't cloud his mind with thoughts of his brothers. Couldn't think about whether the distant screams he'd heard were his brother or his attackers. He'd betrayed both of them, left them for dead so that he could make his escape.

No, he couldn't think about that.

He squeezed on the rudder stick and pushed it forward, turning the boat to the left. The propeller rocketed him down a narrow channel. Looking behind him, he'd hoped that it was too narrow for his pursuers' boat, but they continued, closing the gap between them.

He pressed on down the channel, weaving around corners and avoiding half-submerged logs. Up ahead, he spotted a faint yellow flag tied to a tree. It hung ten feet in the air, right over the dense shoreline.

This is it. This better fucking work.

Letting go of the controls, he snatched his machete and stepped carefully over to the port side. With his foot off the throttle, the engine settled, but the momentum continued to drive the craft forward.

Almost to the flag, Buck leaned over the side of the boat. He spotted his target, a half-inch-thick rope, and locked his gaze on to it. Rearing back the long blade, he swung it as hard as he could. The sharpened steel snapped the tensioned rope with ease, and his follow-through nearly caused him to tumble into the water. Glancing back, he watched as a metal barricade snapped into place just moments after his boat motored past.

He smirked as his pursuers had no choice but to stop in their tracks. Climbing back into the control seat, he hit the gas and turned another corner, leaving them in his wake.

First stage complete.

He was following an outline, an escape route he and his brothers had orchestrated years earlier. It was an "if-all-else-fails" plan, just in case they were ever compromised.

He headed northwest through a maze of narrow, winding channels for half an hour before he hit the end of the line.

Just before the channel ended, he reached a black pool of water that he knew was well over twenty feet deep. When he reached the center of the deep hole, he slowed and drove the bow up onto the muddy shore

206

beside him. Killing the engine, he threw a black duffle bag and a backpack onto a small patch of tall grass, then moved to the transom. Bending down, he pulled the drain plug, allowing water to flow in freely. He threw the plug aside, stepped up onto the bow and vaulted onto the shore.

With a strong push, he shoved the boat out into the center of the pool. Grabbing his bag and duffle, he watched as water filled his airboat. Within minutes, the dark liquid completely engulfed the boat and it disappeared from view.

He stood still for a moment, listening to the silence around him. He thought he could hear something far in the distance, an engine of some kind. They were looking for him, no doubt. They'd called in all the cavalry to take him down. He looked out over the vast swamp. He was miles from his island but was far from being out of the woods yet.

With his backpack secured and the black duffle strapped across his chest, he took off north, trailblazing through thick clusters of trees and swampland. An hour later, he'd traversed all the way to a branch of Shark River, a major tributary that stretches ten miles from Ponce de Leon Bay up into the heart of the Glades.

He headed up along the shoreline for a quarter mile, then dropped his bags, crouched down, and crawled under a thick patch of foliage. Reaching into a narrow gap, he grabbed a plastic handle and pulled a kayak out of its hiding place. There were two others resting beside it that wouldn't be needed. A paddle was secured to its side, and once it was out, he loaded up his gear and slid it into the river.

He paddled eight miles in all, passing the Canepatch historic site and heading up Squawk

Creek. By the time he reached his destination, the sun was starting to set. It had been a hell of a long day. He was exhausted, dehydrated, and hungry.

When the creek died off, he stepped out and pulled the kayak up onto the shore. He climbed out and unloaded his gear. Then, just as he had for his airboat, he sent the kayak to a watery grave by pressing it down, fully submerging the cockpit and letting it sink down toward the center of the river.

He grabbed his gear, trekked three miles east through the swamp, and eventually reached the end of an old service road. Near the base of a rusted radio tower that had long been left to the elements, there was a large camouflage tarp covering a vehicle. Buck removed thick branches that had been used to keep the tarp in place. Lifting it off, he revealed an old Silverado he'd stolen from a junkyard and fixed up years earlier. Having been sitting idle for so long, it didn't start up at first. But Buck had all the tools he needed in the cab, and within an hour, he had the old engine humming.

Phase one and two of the escape plan were complete. Now all he had to do was drive out of the park without getting stopped.

He threw his gear on the passenger seat, climbed in, and shut the door behind him.

No, getting stopped wouldn't mean the end.

He had his revolver and a handful of rounds. He could handle things if he got stopped. Could take care of the situation with a well-placed round. It was getting captured that he feared. He just had to get the hell out of there without getting captured.

He put the truck in drive and hit the gas. He had two miles of neglected backroad to traverse before hitting the main road. It was 2100 and the sky was dark. He just had to keep it together for another hour or so. He glanced at the black duffle bag resting beside him.

Then I need to see about selling this and getting the fuck out of this country.

TWENTY-FIVE

I stood on the edge of the hideout, looking out over the water as they returned on the airboat. Using hand signals, I directed them over to a part of the beach that didn't have a chained-down alligator. Billy was at the controls, and he killed the engine, letting the boat slow naturally and rise up over the muddy shore. I wrapped a hand around the bow and pulled it up even more.

"We were so close to having him," Jack said as he stepped up toward the bow.

Pete shook his head in frustration and glanced over at me. "You call in the feds?"

I nodded. They'd called me on my sat phone just as I was about to call the local police and Coast Guard station. They'd quickly informed me that the final remaining brother had managed to get away and was running northwest toward Shark River.

Jack and Pete leaned over and got their first good look at me.

"Damn, you alright, bro?" Jack said, motioning

210

toward my wounds. Ange had bandaged me up pretty good using a first aid kit Mitch had on his airboat. "Seems like every time I see you, you look worse and worse."

"Well, it looks worse than it is," I said, waving a hand. "Though I might be able to top your forty-five gunshot wound now."

He told me we could compare scars later, then hopped down onto the shore. Pete followed down behind him, then Billy took up the rear. He didn't look like the usual tall, confident guy I'd been accustomed to the past few days. Instead, he was hunched over with his head down.

"I'm sorry, Logan," he said quietly as he passed by me. "We had one job to do and we blew it. I blew it."

I placed a hand on his shoulder.

"Don't worry about it, my friend," I said. "You've been a big help in this. Sometimes you do everything right and the fish still gets off the hook."

He cracked a smile, nodded, and straightened up a little. The four of us headed up into the abandoned hideout.

"What the hell's that?" Jack said, pointing toward the hatch at the center of the camp.

"A tunnel," I said. "Goes down about ten feet or so."

"What's down there?" Pete asked.

"A small living space," I said. "Beds, nonperishable food, and a few hundred pounds of cocaine."

That got all of their attention quick.

Jack's eyes grew wide. "That much? Holy shit, bro."

Pete and Billy both stared in awe for a few

seconds.

"Has Mitch shown up yet?" Pete asked.

I nodded. "He's down there now. Officers from the Monroe County Police Department are on their way, ETA under an hour, with a few detectives as well as EODs to take care of the explosives. They're also sending two boats up Shark River since that's the direction he was heading. And I also called the Guard over on Islamorada. They're sending two choppers to look for our lost Gladesman."

"Good," Pete said with a nod. "What's the plan now for us?"

"We leave," Ange said, climbing up out of the hatch. "Before we get stuck in a small room for hours on end answering question after question." She walked over, wrapped an arm around me, and added, "Plus, we need to get you to a doctor. After you take a shower."

I cracked a smile and looked down at my bandaged-up shoulder and chest.

"I think you did a pretty good job of taking care of it," I said. "I don't see any need to go to a hospital."

I shot her my best smile, hoping she'd fall for it.

"Fine," she said. "You win. I'll stitch it up myself on the boat ride home. But we gotta at least get Dr. Patel to make a house call. I'm sure you'll need a rabies shot now."

"Agreed," I said, knowing that it was as good of a compromise as I was gonna get.

Though I understood their obvious importance and they'd brought me back from down and out a handful of times in my life, I couldn't stand hospitals. I think it's the smell of them more than anything.

"Rabies?" Jack said, raising an eyebrow at me.

"What the hell did you pick a fight with?"

"A German Shepherd," I said. "A big one. That reminds me, how's the pooch doing?"

"Still sleeping like a baby," Ange replied. "We got him secured for when he wakes up. We'll need to get him transported and taken to an animal shelter."

I nodded. It would be a long and difficult road to bring that dog back to normalcy.

"A German Shepherd," Jack said, shaking his head. "You're right. That might top my forty-five wound."

We fell silent for a moment, and Pete looked around the group. "So if we leave, who will Mitch say did all this?"

There was a slight pause.

"Billy," I said. "You mind taking the credit for this one? After all, I never would've been able to track that brother down if it wasn't for you."

He was taken aback. He looked around at the group, stunned.

"I barely did anything," he said. "I can't take credit for something I didn't do."

"I don't want to force you to do anything you're not comfortable with. But you'd be doing us a big favor."

"But people should know who did this. This is a big story, and you're heroes for bringing these men down."

"We don't like the attention," I said. "But if you don't either, I understand. We can just say Mitch spotted something suspicious on the island."

"Spotted something suspicious," Jack said, "then snuck onto the island, killed a gator, cleared a tripwire, took down an attack dog, and killed a murderer?"

I laughed, then stopped myself as the pain in my chest and shoulder hit me.

"I'm sure you guys can think of something," I said.

Billy paused a moment, then nodded.

"Alright," he said. "You've all done so much, it's the least I can do."

"Great," I said, thanking him and patting him on the back. I turned to the others and added, "Already cleared it with Mitch, so let's get out of here."

"Heading home and resting for a few days is a good idea," Pete said. "This killer's been spooked out of his cave, and he'll need to venture into society at some point. We'll give the authorities a chance to take him down."

"And if they don't?" Jack said. "What if he gets away? He stopped us with some kind of spring-loaded gate mechanism thing. He had his escape planned out."

We paused a moment. Atticus scurried off into the shrubs and came back holding a stick. He dropped it at my feet, then looked up expectantly.

"Not here, boy," I said with a smile. "But first thing when we get home."

"If by some miracle he manages to escape," Ange said, "it's not like he's overflowing with options."

I nodded. "Alright, time to get out of here. These killers have taken up enough of our time, and a bar of soap, a cold beer, and a nap are all calling my name."

"Billy, you mind if we borrow your boat?" Pete said. "We'll leave it at Flamingo."

"No problem," he said. "My boat is your boat. I'll ride back with Mitch."

Everyone climbed back onto the airboat, and I

called over Atticus, who was looking for another stick in the middle of the hideout. I was the last to board, and before I did, I turned back to Billy.

"Thanks for everything, Billy," I said, shaking his hand. "Really, we couldn't have taken them down without you." We exchanged a few nods and knowing glances. "You'll keep us informed if you learn anything about the last brother?"

"Of course," he replied.

I took a step toward the airboat, then turned back.

"Your family line has a proud history," I said. "I think Osceola would be proud of you as well. You're a good man, Billy."

He smiled, and I turned and clasped hands with Ange, who helped me up onto the boat.

TWENTY-SIX

We kept a low profile, avoiding any possible confrontations with police and Coast Guard as we motored down the Watson and across Whitewater Bay. We navigated down Buttonwood Canal and reached Flamingo just as the sun was beginning to set.

We grabbed a quick bite to eat at the food truck just as it was about to close. Having a hot, well-prepared meal was incredible after living the past few days on MREs and jerky. It reminded me of all of the camping trips and missions I'd gone on over the years. Fresh, hot food never tastes better than after spending time out in the wild.

We ran into Hank Boggs as we were heading back over to the ocean side of the marina. He actually said that he was happy to see me in one piece, which caused me to raise an eyebrow. When I asked him why he was so happy, he motioned toward his airboat. He had a dead wild hog lying in the bow.

Pete and Jack agreed to take the Baia back to

Key West while Ange and I hopped into the Cessna. Atticus jumped onto the dock, then vaulted into the cockpit without a word.

"Guess you guys got Atty," Jack said with a laugh.

Ange started up the engine and motored us out into Florida Bay. We took off into a partially clouded sky with the sun setting to our right. It was beautiful—wide streaks of orange and red hues. The water beneath us glistened like diamonds. Western clouds turned dark purple with bright glowing edges.

I've always loved watching the sunset, seeing it transition and shift to various patterns of color with every passing second. As I watched nature's work of art unfold, I thought about the past few days. From the moment Jack had told us about the Shepherds' murder at our underwater hotel in Key Largo, we'd experienced a whirlwind of activity. We'd been swept up into a dangerous and difficult chase through one of the harshest terrains on earth. And we'd managed to pull through together.

But one uncomfortable thought continued to linger. The final Harlan brother. He'd managed to slip through our fingers. I reasoned that there was a slim-to-nothing chance that he'd make it out of that swamp without being caught. But, he and his brothers had proven over and over that they were smarter than they'd appeared. That they had tricks up their sleeves and plans for when shit hit the fan.

I glanced over at Ange. She turned her head and smiled at me. She'd changed into a blue tank top before taking off, and she had her blond hair pulled back and wore a pair of aviator sunglasses. One look at her made me forget all about the killer that got away. There was nothing I could do about that, but what I could do was enjoy the moment I was in. Sitting beside the most beautiful and amazing woman on earth, who just so happened to be my wife.

"You doing good?" she said.

I grabbed her hand and nodded.

"Never better."

Atticus jumped up into my lap, licked my face, then looked out through the copilot window. He seemed to be enjoying the view as much as I was.

Leaning forward, I gazed down at the beautiful island chain I'd called home for the past year and a half. I was happy to be returning to my paradise on earth and the only tropical destination in the continental United States.

We splashed down in Tarpon Cove twenty minutes later. After tying off, we loaded our stuff into my Tacoma, which was still parked in the lot. The island was dark as we made the short drive to my house on Palmetto Street. Atticus jumped out as soon as the door opened, running off to explore and smell everything in the yard.

Inside, we both dropped our bags and let out a big sigh of relief. First things first—I stepped into the master bathroom and started up the shower. As the water warmed up, I looked up and saw my reflection in the mirror above the sink. It was the first time I'd seen myself in over forty-eight hours. I had dirt caked on the corners of my face, my beard was scruffy, and my brown hair was messy as hell. I also had a few scratches across my neck and cheeks, most of which were due to trekking through miles of razor-sharp sawgrass.

As the mirror started steaming up, I slid out of my dirty, sticky clothes and stepped into the shower. The warm water felt incredible as it splashed against my sore and aching body. I leaned over and looked down as it dripped down my face and splashed at my feet. The water was dirty for a few minutes as all of the accumulated grime from the past few days gave way.

I spent a glorious half hour in the spraying heat before cutting off the water and stepping out. I dried off, then opened the door and moved into the master bedroom with my towel wrapped around my waist. Ange had gathered some medical supplies on the living room table and was sitting on the couch, reading something on her phone. Her eyes darted up as I stepped into view.

"All fresh and clean," she said as I walked over and went in for a short but passionate kiss. "Hubba-hubba. Even though you stank, I have to admit that there was something hot about your rough wild man look."

I smiled, and we moved out back through the sliding glass door. I lit a row of tiki torches while Ange cleaned my wounds and stitched me up out on the balcony. Atticus ran up the porch stairs with a drool-covered tennis ball in his mouth. In between the stitching, I tossed it down across my backyard a few times, making him the happiest dog in the world.

Just as Ange was finishing up, we heard a car pull up into the driveway. I was a cautious guy by nature. I'd also pissed off a lot of bad guys in my time. As a result, I'd installed an impressive state-of-the-art security system after I'd bought the house. But I realized at that moment that I hadn't switched it back on since I'd disarmed it upon our arrival.

"Relax," Ange said, seeing that I was running over things in my mind. "It's just some dinner. I didn't feel like cooking, so I ordered it while you were in the shower."

She smiled and winked at me, then headed inside. Less than a minute later, she returned with a big pizza box. After a few slices of supreme, we headed inside and Ange mixed up two Long Island iced teas.

"Trying to get me drunk?" I said.

She laughed and handed me one. "As if I need to."

We barely finished the drink before embracing and staggering into the master bedroom. She flipped on some Gary Allen, and before long, there really was nothing on but the radio. We were all tangled up in the sheets and made love twice before passing out to the sound of the wind rustling the palm leaves and the water lapping against the sea wall.

TWENTY-SEVEN

Buck Harlan drove down the rough backroad, maneuvering over fallen branches, bouncing up and down, and splashing through muddy puddles. It was dark, and he had to keep it slow to avoid crashing into the occasional obstacle.

Finally, he covered the two miles of neglected dirt road and reached Main Park Road. That section of State Road 9336 stretched from the Ernest F. Cole Visitor Center nearly forty miles down to the Flamingo Visitor Center.

Buck eased on the brakes and idled for a few seconds. He looked left, then right. Seeing no other headlights, he pulled out and turned left, heading toward the entrance into the park. He had his radio set to the AM emergency station. After driving a few miles down the paved road, he heard an emergency report through the old crackling speakers. It was a replay of a report they'd apparently made earlier that day.

"Suspect is considered armed and dangerous,"

the voice said. "Forty-year-old Caucasian male. Approximately six feet tall. Three hundred pounds. Dressed in ragged clothes. If you have any information regarding this suspect, contact the Monroe County Police Department at…"

Then the message repeated itself twice before the station crackled back to the normal news of the day. Buck motored for ten minutes longer before making a wide, sweeping turn and driving onto a long straightaway.

Suddenly, he spotted something unusual up ahead and slammed on the brakes.

Shit. Holy fucking shit.

He switched off the headlights and peered through the windshield. Up ahead about half a mile, he could see the entrance to the park. The only problem was, he could also see a group of police cars parked and officers standing beside the shack with flashlights. It was clear that they were inspecting any and all vehicles that were leaving the park. Buck had thought of everything so far. Had been ready for each step of the escape plan. But he wasn't ready for this. He could hold his own, but not against a group of armed police officers.

A sudden flash appeared in his rearview mirror. Another car had turned onto the straightaway and was quickly approaching his position from a few miles in the distance. He needed to make a decision. He needed to move.

A moment later, he hit the gas, turned around and cruised back the way he had come for less than a minute before turning south down a road that led to a few trailheads and another visitor center. He knew the park as well as anyone alive and knew that the Anhinga Trail would be his best bet.

He reached a small empty lot at the end of the road. Wanting to keep his truck hidden from view, he drove off-road and parked behind a storage shed. Turning off the engine, he flipped off the headlights, grabbed his gear, and stepped out. He followed the trail until it started to loop back around, then stepped down into the swamp.

After half a mile of trekking east in the wet, muddy darkness, he reached a large government compound. It was a sprawling patch of cleared land littered with travel trailers, manufactured homes, and tents, all of it run by the Florida National Parks Association. It was where the rangers, maintenance workers, and various other temporary and full-time federal employees called home while working in the parks. But for Buck, the best thing about the place was that it was located outside the park, just past the entrance and the police inspection.

Being summer, the slow season in the Glades, most of the spaces were vacant and most of the homes empty. Buck kept to the shadows as he headed toward a travel trailer near the back edge of the compound. There was light emanating from inside and a park ranger SUV parked in the gravel lot beside it.

He crouched down beside the trailer, then peeked through one of the side windows. There was a middle-aged woman inside, sitting at the table staring at her laptop. Buck waited a few seconds to make sure that she was alone, then headed for the door.

Dropping his gear onto the grass, he snatched his revolver and stood right in front of the door. He gave two raps with his knuckles. Not so loud as to sound threatening, not so quiet as to sound suspicious. He was hoping that she'd open the door without taking a look first. If she looked, he'd be forced to resort to plan B.

He saw fingers, followed by a set of eyes peering through the blinds.

Plan B it is.

Buck raised his revolver into her line of sight, aiming the barrel straight at her face.

"Open the door or you die," he mouthed without making a sound.

Her hands shook and her mouth dropped open. She hesitated for a moment, and Buck could tell that she was struggling to make a decision.

He moved his face closer, mouthed the words again, then pulled back the hammer. The door clicked, then slowly swung open.

"Grab my shit and load it into your car," he said quietly, motioning toward the two bags resting in the grass.

She frantically grabbed her keys from the counter beside her. She wasn't even wearing shoes, but she did as he said. She loaded up everything into the back of the SUV, then stood for a moment, her body shaking in fear.

"Now you're going to drive me out of here," he said. "If anyone stops us, you make something up. If you say a word about me or give away that I'm here, you're dead."

TWENTY-EIGHT

The next morning, we climbed aboard my twenty-two-foot Robalo center-console and motored over to the Conch Harbor Marina. I kept it stored in a small boathouse right on the channel in my backyard. I prefer it to my truck from time to time. It takes a little longer but is much more scenic and fun, and there's usually less traffic.

It was just after 0800 when we cruised into the marina. The sky was mostly clear, the water calm, and it was already eighty degrees. But it felt a hell of a lot better than the Glades heat given the nice cool ocean breeze.

Ange tied us off next to the Baia at slip twenty-four, then we climbed up onto the dock. Jack and Pete were talking to Gus over near the office but headed over our way when they saw us.

"I'm surprised you're up," I said to Jack when they walked within earshot. "I was expecting to have to dump this on you to get you out of bed," I added, holding up a bag of ice I'd brought from my house.

225

Jack was notorious for his sleeping in. That combined with the fact that he refused to wear a wristwatch resulted in my dragging him out of bed at least a few times a month.

"I took care of it half an hour ago," Pete said with a laugh.

"Hey, after what we just went through in the Glades, don't we deserve a little rest?"

I laughed. "You can rest out on the water. I need my lobster fix."

The eight-month lobster season in the Keys runs from the beginning of August until the end of March. I'd already missed the first few weeks, so I was anxious to make up for lost time.

"Aren't you supposed to be recovering, bro?"

Jack motioned at my recently stitched-up wounds.

"I think a little light exercise might do me good," I said, glancing over at Ange, who just shook her head.

"That's gonna be quite the scar," Jack said.

He was right. The big attack dog had scratched me good. I'd have a full paw's scar right across the right side of my chest when all was said and done.

"You guys see my baby?" Pete said with a big grin on his face.

Ange and I looked at him in confusion, so he turned and motioned toward the parking lot. I drew my gaze down the dock and spotted a beautiful red '69 Camaro with black stripes. Pete had been working on it for the past few months, and even from that far away I could tell that it was a head turner.

"It looks great, Pete," Ange said.

"Yes, it does," I added. "Hard to believe that's the same rusted car I used to see under a tarp behind your restaurant."

"She's a beauty alright," Pete said. "And she's running as good as ever. Now I just need to take her someplace where I can really stretch her legs. The Keys have more cops per capita than a donut shop."

We all couldn't help but laugh at that.

I climbed aboard the Baia alongside Ange with Atticus right on our heels. Grabbing my cooler from the galley, I lifted open the lid and poured in the ice. I threw in a few beers, coconut waters, and bottles of water, then lugged it up to the main deck. We gathered our gear for the day while Ange blended up a mango-banana smoothie for breakfast. We untied the lines, started up the Baia's twin 600-hp engines, and motored out of the marina while sipping the delicious frozen concoction.

"Either of you heard anything from Mitch?" Pete asked.

"Not since the island," Ange said. "What about you?"

"No, but I just got off the phone with Billy."

"And?" I asked.

Judging by his brief silence, I figured the news wasn't good.

"They haven't found him yet," Pete said. "The choppers flew back and forth for hours. Never even saw an airboat anywhere out that way."

"What about Shark River?" I asked. "Police said they were sending a few boats to see if he made the crossing."

Pete shook his head. "Came up dry there too. The guy disappeared. Like a ghost. But they're keeping after it. They've got a police inspection at the park's main entrance to make sure he doesn't get out that way. I'm sure they'll find him. He's gotta be

227

somewhere—if he's still alive, that is."

"Probably won't get far," Jack said. "Even if he gets out of the swamps, he's still screwed. Didn't strike me as a guy with a lot of extra money lying around, and he can't sell his coke. He left the haul down in their bunker house thing."

"Maybe," Pete said. "Or maybe he just took as much as he could carry and left the rest. Which would mean he's now gonna try and sell it as quickly as he can."

We fell silent for a moment.

"Makes sense," I said. "If that's the case, I'm sure he'll try and sell it to whoever he's been working with over the years."

We shifted our thoughts and conversation to happier topics as we neared the end of the no-wake zone.

"Alright, Jack," I said. "Where are we heading?"

He smiled and grabbed a cardboard tube from his bag. Uncapping the top, he pulled out a roll of paper that was probably his most prized possession on earth. It contained our location of go-to bug sites. What we liked to do was hit up the well-known sites first, then shift over to our secret sites as the season dragged on. It was our own little system to ensure that we never came back from a day on the water without a livewell full of our daily limits.

"Let's do the Kremlin," he said.

Our fathers had named the site the Kremlin years ago, since part of the rock and reef formations bear a resemblance to Saint Basil's Cathedral.

Jack leaned forward and punched the coordinates into the GPS without bothering for a reply.

Jack was a fourth-generation conch, and if he decided on a site for the day, I had no place to object.

I'd also dived for lobster at the Kremlin a few times before and always enjoyed the cluster of patch reefs.

Once clear of the harbor, I hit the throttles and rocketed us into the Atlantic side. We cracked open a few Paradise Sunset beers, cranked up the satellite radio, and leaned back. The sun on my face and the ocean wind in my hair gave me a high-on-life feeling that was tough to beat.

We reached our destination twenty minutes later. After dropping and setting the anchor, I killed the engine and we excitedly donned our gear. Even though lobster season was young, there were only a handful of other boats in sight, and the closest one was a quarter of a mile south near the main reef.

Once ready, we grabbed our tools of the trade: tickle sticks, aluminum lobster gauges, nets, mesh bags, and gloves. Pressing my mask snug against my face, I flipped backward and splashed into the warm, clear tropical water. I had my long free diving fins, allowing me to reach the bottom twenty feet below with just a few smooth kicks.

Lobster like to hide under whatever they can find, usually the edges of reefs, rocks, or other structures. The key is to look for their antennae, which stick out from their hiding places and give away their position. I finned for thirty seconds along the bottom, then spotted a few under the edge of the reef.

Moving close, I held my net in place, then prodded them out with my tickle stick. Two bugs whooshed out and swam right into my net. One was obviously too small, but I grabbed the other with my gloved right hand and measured its carapace length. Three inches is the legal minimum, and this guy was three and a quarter, so I stowed him away in my mesh bag.

I bagged two more before turning back to the boat and surfacing. There are few things I enjoy as much as spending a day out on the water, hunting down lobster. I'm in love with the tropical underwater world. The colors, the incredible variation of marine life, the silence of it all. It's like meditation or going to church. I guess everybody has their own kind of escape, or means of returning to their true selves. I've never been a religious man, but being in a place this extraordinary makes it difficult to believe that there isn't some kind of master artist behind the scenes. The world we live in can be beautiful beyond comprehension, and I always feel an overwhelming sense of gratitude every time I drop beneath the waves. I always feel lucky to be able to drop down at least one more time.

After hours in the water, we all climbed out and admired our day's catch. We all easily reached our daily limit of six and were able to choose only the biggest ones to harvest. We cleaned and cooked up a few bugs right there on the deck using my portable grill. While lounging and enjoying the fruits of our labor, we spoke animatedly about what we'd seen.

"I'm surprised you didn't spear that hogfish," Ange said, nudging me on the shoulder. "It was plenty big and swam right past us."

I shrugged. "Maybe next time."

"Don't worry," Pete said while toweling off and playing with Atticus on the sunbed. "Hogfish are like deer crossing the road. There's always more than one."

"Or serial killers in the Everglades," Jack said with a grin.

After filling our stomachs to our heart's content,

we splashed back into the water for some spearfishing. By early afternoon, I had my livewell and two coolers full of the ocean's bounties.

TWENTY-NINE

Previous Evening
Upper Keys

Just before midnight, the park ranger SUV pulled up to the gate of a dark boatyard on the Florida Bay side of Tavernier. The place was surrounded by a high fence with curled razor wire on top. It was small and out of the way. There were a few dilapidated boats on the hard. One sailboat was tied off to a neglected dock that was missing many of its planks.

A skinny guy with dreadlocks stepped out the side door of a small rusted warehouse. He walked right over to the gate and was about to tell his visitor to piss off when Buck rolled down the window and leaned out.

"What the hell are you doing here?" Dreadlocks asked, freezing in his tracks. He was young. Maybe mid-twenties. He looked at the side of the SUV, reading the words. "And what the—"

"Just shut up and open the gate," Buck snapped.

"I've got a delivery."

The young guy stared with wide eyes for a few seconds. They'd developed a certain system, a standard way of handling business between their group and the reclusive Gladesmen. This wasn't the way their business was supposed to be conducted.

Dreadlocks shook his head. "Darby isn't going to like this."

"He's going to like this," Buck growled, grabbing the black duffle on the seat beside him and hoisting it into view. "Now open the damn gate."

He took a step back, then raised a finger, signaling for Buck to wait a minute. He reached into his pocket, pulled out a cellphone, then pressed a speed dial number. He moved a few more steps away from the gate so Buck couldn't hear his conversation. Less than thirty seconds after grabbing his phone, he hung up and moved back over to the fence.

He replaced the cellphone with a jingling set of keys in his pocket, then unlocked the gate. In the distance, Buck could see one of the warehouse's garage doors rise up.

"Pull into the warehouse," the young guy said after pulling the squeaky gate open.

Buck flipped the guy off as he accelerated past. He rolled into the dark warehouse, stopped beside a black Chrysler 300, then killed the engine. The manually operated garage door slammed shut behind him. Dim light bled in from a nearby office window. Aside from that, the place was pitch black.

He turned to look at Martha in the backseat. She had duct tape pressed tight to her mouth. It wrapped around her head twice, flattening her dark curly hair to the back of her neck. Buck had cut off the backseat nylon seat belts and used the strong fabric to bind her wrists and ankles together.

"Not a sound out of you," he said.

He grabbed the duffle bag and stepped out. It took a moment for his eyes to adjust in the darkness. The guy who'd operated the garage door was at his back, but Buck didn't even acknowledge him. Instead, the rough killer strode confidently straight into a small office.

There was an old leather couch on one side. Two women lay on it, smoke rising from a few old joints resting in a tray on the table beside them. An old white guy with wrinkled skin and colorful tattoos up his neck sat at a desk. It was clear aside from a stack of papers and a ballpoint pen.

The old guy rose right as Buck walked through the door.

"Well, Bucky," the old guy said. "You're having a bad fucking day."

His voice was raspy, the product of years of inhaling tobacco fumes.

"I don't have time for small talk, Darby," Buck said. He walked over to the desk and dropped the duffle bag right in the old guy's face. "There's twenty pounds there. That's two hundred big ones if you want it. Now"—Buck leaned over the desk and narrowed his gaze—"fork over the cash so I can get the hell out of here."

Darby stared with unflinching eyes back at Buck. After a lifetime of crime, he wasn't intimidated easily. He leaned back in his chair, stuck his tongue against the inside of his cheek, and shook his head.

"You don't know your place, redneck," he replied.

He raised a hand and snapped his fingers.

In an instant, the young guy with dreadlocks

appeared in the doorway. The two women sat up on the couch and stared at Buck.

"You come storming into my house unannounced," Darby said. "Desperation oozing out of your fat body. You'll take twenty grand for the coke. That's the discounted rate for pissing me off."

There was a brief moment of silence. The two hardened men stood facing each other as if engaged in a Wild West standoff. The tension in the room was so thick it made it difficult to breathe.

Buck gritted his teeth, then raised his hands in the air and lowered his head.

"Where's the money?" Buck said, agreeing to the new deal.

Darby shot Buck an evil smile. He swiveled his leather chair around and opened the safe behind him. Grabbing a stack, he turned around and dropped it on the desk.

Buck extended his right hand before Darby could lock up the safe. The old guy hesitated a moment, then accepted.

"You always were a terrible businessman," Darby said. "Consider this the end of our working relationship."

As soon as Buck's hand slipped away, he snatched the pen from the desk and stabbed it into Darby's left eyeball. The small tip sank deep into the soft, gooey organ. Blood dripped out and Darby's head jerked back. He let out a shrill cry and pressed his hands up to his face.

With the smooth, quick action of a trained killer, Buck snatched the revolver from his hip. He spun around and put a bullet through Dreadlocks first. The young guy was raising a handgun of his own when the lead struck his chest and knocked his body back through the door frame behind him. The two women on the couch screamed for only a brief moment before being silenced by two more quick shots.

Darby continued to yell and curse as blood dripped down his face, splashing onto the weathered wood surface and staining the papers. He reached for the shotgun he kept stowed under the desk. Just as his hands gripped the handle, Buck wrapped his left hand around his neck and jerked his body up over the desk. The shotgun rattled to the concrete floor. Darby looked up in desperation, the pen still stuck halfway into his face.

"You should have taken my offer," Buck grunted. "Now, I'm taking everything."

Buck slammed the handle of his revolver against his ear. Darby let out another yell and continued to shake from shock and pain. He was an experienced drug dealer, but he'd made one very costly mistake. He'd underestimated the power of desperation.

Buck stormed around the desk, kicking the shotgun across the room. He unzipped the duffle bag and emptied out all the coke onto the floor. Then he replaced the drugs with stacks of cash. He loaded up everything in the safe as well as the twenty thousand on the counter, then zipped it back up.

Throwing the bag over his shoulder, he looked down at Darby, watching as he struggled to breathe in a pool of his own blood.

"Consider this the end of our working relationship," Buck said.

The old guy looked up at Buck, dark red covering half of his face.

Buck raised his revolver a few inches, then pulled the trigger, sending a round exploding into the struggling man's forehead. Buck gave a sinister smile

236

as his head turned into a grotesque mess of blood, skin, and bone.

Casually, Buck wiped his brow and holstered his revolver. He crouched down, searched Darby's pockets, and snatched a ring of keys. Grabbing the duffle, he strode back to the door, stepped over Dreadlocks' lifeless body, and headed to the Chrysler parked beside the park ranger SUV.

He set the cash-filled duffle in the passenger seat, then popped open the trunk. Stepping back over to the SUV, he pulled open the side door and grabbed Martha by her shoulder forcefully.

"Get out," he said sternly.

She shifted over and he practically pulled her down to the ground. He forced her into the trunk. She could barely fit in the fetal position, and before Buck slammed the door, he reminded her that if she made any noise, she'd be dead.

Once the trunk was shut, he opened the garage door, then plopped down in the driver's seat and started up the engine. Putting it in reverse, he backed out, then flicked on the headlights. At the entrance, he hit the gas and broke through the gate. He drove toward US-1 but pulled over to the curb of a side street before turning onto it.

He didn't know why he'd pulled over. Glancing to his right, he stared at the duffle bag, which contained over a hundred grand in cash. The best move would be to make a break for Mexico. To get in the car and drive around the Gulf.

The engine was running. It hummed in front of him. All he had to do was hop on the road and turn left, so why couldn't he?

Their faces—he couldn't get them out of his mind. He saw his brothers as clearly as if they were still alive. They haunted him from the grave and drove him mad. But they weren't the only faces he saw.

There was also the guy who'd been responsible for everything. Logan fucking Dodge, the guy he'd wrestled with in Hells Bay. The one who'd tracked them down, discovered their hideout, and rained hell upon him and his brothers.

He needed to make things right. To settle the score. He needed to avenge his brothers' deaths.

He sat in silence, thinking back to his radio conversation with Eli Hutt. It took him a minute, but then it all came back to him.

Logan Dodge. Lives in Key West. Keeps his boat at Conch Harbor Marina.

His foot pressed the gas pedal. He drove forward, then turned onto US-1, heading south.

238

THIRTY

We weighed anchor at 1400 and motored back toward Key West. The wind had picked up to four knots, but the sky was mostly clear and it was still a beautiful day out on the water. Ange was wearing a turquoise bikini and lying on a sprawled-out towel up on the bow. Jack was napping on the sunbed behind me, and Pete was sitting at the dinette, going over a few underwater pictures he'd taken.

As I piloted us past the Eastern Dry Rocks, I heard a sharp whistle. Turning my head, I spotted a white-hulled Privateer Pilothouse roughly a quarter mile off our port bow. There was a guy dressed in full scuba gear standing on the boat's swim platform. He whistled again, then waved at us.

Ange propped herself on an elbow. Her bronzed skin was covered in oil and sparkled under the tropical sun. She turned back to look at me through a pair of dark sunglasses and laughed.

I was used to such behavior. Being married to a woman as beautiful as Ange means I've witnessed a whole lot of guys giving her attention. Whistles, waves, *hey babys*—they're all part of the deal. They almost always lay off when they find out she's married. Rarely do I have to step in and tell the unwanted solicitor to take a hike.

I turned the wheel slightly to starboard and picked up speed.

She's not interested, pal.

I laughed and smiled back at Ange.

"Hey, that's Cal!" Jack said over the roar of the engines and the gusts of wind.

I turned back to look at my friend, watched as he sat up on the sunbed. Looking back over the port gunwale, I saw that the diver was still waving and whistling away. I eased back on the throttles, wondering if maybe his friend was in trouble of some kind.

Jack waved back, then slid his bare feet onto the deck beside him.

"Logan, turn around, bro," Jack said, moving his lean frame effortlessly up beside me. "That's Cal Brooks. Looks like he found something."

I eased us down to thirty knots, then performed a big, sweeping turn.

"He owns the Conch Republic Dive Shop, right?" I said.

"Yeah. We've known each other for years. He operates out of Boot Key."

I nodded. I'd met Cal once or twice in passing at various places in the islands. His charter was small but had a good reputation.

I motored over alongside Cal's boat, *Zig-Zag*, then idled the engines. A young guy wearing a Panama hat was at the helm of the privateer. The main deck had been customized to take out diving groups, with benches on the sides and tank holders against the transom. Cal was still standing on the swim platform. He was a short middle-aged man with an impressive belly.

"What's up, Cali?" Jack said. "You need me to help set up your dive gear for you? That second stage goes in your mouth, by the way."

Cal had his mask hanging around his neck and his regulator hanging over his shoulder.

"No, I was gonna offer some carbs for your bony ass," he retaliated. "This breeze is gonna take you with it any second."

Jack laughed. "No charter today?"

"Nope. Just out for fun. I called you guys over 'cause an eagle ray just swam by."

Jack turned to look over at me, his eyes wide. The large majestic fish was one of Jack's favorites.

"Hey, Logan," Cal said. "Good to see you. The ray was swimming south when we saw it just a few minutes ago."

I told him it was good to see him too, then thanked him.

"Having dinner at Joe's later if you guys wanna join us," he said as we motored off.

Sloppy Joes was a landmark in Key West. The bar and restaurant had been a favorite hangout spot of Hemingway, who'd owned a house just down the street from it.

Jack thanked Cal again, then I accelerated us south. After a few minutes, Ange shouted from the bow.

"There it is!" she said, pointing down at the water.

I glanced at the dash. We were only in about thirty feet of water. It would make sense for one of us to stay at the controls rather than drop anchor.

"I'll take the helm on this one," Pete said, reading my mind.

We switched places and he used the fish finder to track the ray. In less than a minute, we had our fins on and our masks strapped. We splashed down ahead of the ray and finned toward the bottom. Jack had been smart and pocketed a few dive weights. Combined with his zero body fat, he sank to the bottom like a rock.

Moments after we reached the sandy seafloor, the massive ray came soaring into view like a B-2 stealth bomber with white spots. Spotted eagle rays are usually seen in shallower waters in the Keys, gliding along while slowly flapping their large pectoral fins, which jut out like wings. They can grow up to nine feet long and eight feet wide and can weigh over five hundred pounds.

The incredible creature swam right by us, then continued on, gliding right over a shallow patch reef. It was a breathtaking sight. I'd seen eagle rays before, but never that close. With the show over, we looked around briefly at the sand and seagrass around us, then finned for the surface. I made a mental note to buy Cal a drink that night at Joe's as I broke the surface.

"How awesome was that?" Jack said.

"That was enormous," Ange added.

We swam over to the Baia, which was idling beside us. Pete was at the helm, but he wasn't looking at us. He had the radio pressed up against his ear and was staring through the windscreen. As we neared the boat, he turned around and lowered the radio.

"I got Jane on the line," he said.

Jane Verona was with the Key West Police

Department. She'd been chosen as the temporary sheriff until the city went about picking a replacement for Charles Wilkes. Charles, a career homefront patriot and a good friend of mine, had been killed by Carson and her Darkwater thugs four months ago.

"What is it?" I said.

Pete paused a moment. He looked uncomfortable.

"It's not good," he said.

I didn't even bother moving over to the swim platform. I kicked, wrapped my hands over the top of the starboard gunwale, and pulled myself up out of the water in one quick motion. Sliding out of my fins, I set them on the deck. Pete cranked up the radio's volume, allowing us to hear the thirty-six-year-old Latina.

"I've got everyone listening in, Jane," Pete said. "What happened?"

"There's been a serious incident in Tavernier," she said. Her tone was hard, her voice articulate even through the radio speaker. "Four people were murdered at Blue Sky Boatyard." She paused a moment, letting the information sink in. "It's clear that the assailant is the same guy you tracked down in the Everglades. Buck Harlan."

I shook my head, then looked out over the water. I'd had a bad feeling deep in my gut ever since he'd escaped on his airboat the previous day. At once, the worst-case scenario became a reality.

"Who were the victims, Jane?" Pete asked.

"From the looks of things, a group of drug dealers that law enforcement has been tracking here for some time now. Looks like this Buck guy was here to make a deal. For one reason or another, shit hit the fan. Then Buck left his stacks of cocaine and

243

made off with a safe full of cash."

Holy shit.

We went quiet a moment. Ange moved over and sat down beside me.

"Guess you were right about the coke, Pete," she said.

"It gets worse," Jane said. "I talked to Mitch Ross from the parks service, and he told me that the ranger vehicle at the scene of the crime was issued to Martha Green. Mitch said that she didn't show up to work this morning and that she wasn't in her trailer."

I pictured the woman in my mind and gritted my teeth in anger. I'd just seen her the previous day at the visitor center in Flamingo. It didn't look good for her. If by some miracle she was still alive, she'd be in bad shape.

Pete looked down at the deck and said, "Wait a minute, if he left the vehicle, how did he get out of there? He take one from the guys he killed?"

"Looks that way," Jane said. "And we don't know where he went after that. We have teams on the loose, looking everywhere for him. We also have a police inspection on US-1 in Key Largo. Coast Guard's on alert as well. We'll get him, you guys. We have to get him."

Pete lowered the radio, then glanced over at us.

"So this asshole not only makes it out," Jack said, "but he kidnaps a park ranger in the process, then murders a bunch of people." He shook his head. "Can this guy's rap sheet get any damn longer?"

He was standing with his back to the transom, hands on his hips. We were all upset, and rightfully so. I'd felt a surge of anger swell up during the call but had quelled it and was running everything over in my mind logically.

I stood up, grabbed a towel from the dinette seat, and handed it to Ange.

"It's time we finished what we started," I said. "The longer this guy stays alive, the more people are gonna die."

Ange nodded as she toweled off. "Agreed."

"At least the feds have geography to their advantage," Pete said. "There's only one road in or out of the Keys. He might have a hard time with their blockade."

"Unless he hauled ass out of here right after killing those people," Jack said, playing devil's advocate. "If that's the case, he could be anywhere."

"The only reason he could have to come here would be to get that money," Ange said. "He's probably gonna try and make a run for South America, right, Logan?"

"One step at a time," I said, striding over to the helm. "Everybody hold on."

I hit the throttles, accelerating us back toward Key West.

THIRTY-ONE

I piloted us back into the marina, killed the engines, and tied off to slip twenty-four. After a quick cleanup and gathering of gear, Jack and Pete hauled our day's catch onto the dock and carried it down to the cleaning station. As they did, Ange and I went quickly to work rinsing our gear with the freshwater hose.

I thought about Buck the whole trip back. We'd tracked him down in the swamps, where he'd had the home court advantage. Now, he'd ventured out into the real world. After spending over ten years living in the middle of nowhere, I knew that adjusting to normal society wouldn't be the easiest thing. We had the advantage now, and I knew that it would only be a matter of time before we tracked him down again.

I looked up and saw Gus Henderson approach from the direction of the marina office. He was wearing an orange visor, sunglasses, and a Conch Republic tee shirt. He flip-flopped past Jack and Pete and stopped right beside the Baia.

"Feel free to as much of that as you want, Gus," I said, motioning toward the fish and lobster the guys were hauling over to the cleaning station.

"I need to talk to you about something," he said flatly.

He motioned down the dock, indicating that he wanted our conversation to be private. Intrigued, I set my rinsed gear on the sunbed, then stepped onto the dock and followed him a few strides away from the nearest boat.

"Somebody called the office asking for you, Logan," he said.

He spoke in a serious tone, which was unusual for the marina owner. I raised my eyebrows, tilting my head so that my eyes could meet his. His gaze was narrowed on me, his brow furrowed.

"At first he said that he was an old friend of yours. But I figured it was a lie from the start. He gave off a strange vibe, even over the phone."

"What did he want, Gus?" I said.

"At first he asked what slip you were at. But I don't give out personal information like that to anyone. I protect my patrons." He paused a moment, clearing his throat. "Then the conversation turned sour. His tone shifted and he raised his voice. He told me to relay a message to you. He said that he wants you to meet him over at Sugarloaf Landing. He also said that if you don't come alone, he'll kill her. Didn't say who she was, though."

I paused a moment, taking in everything he'd said. My right hand unconsciously formed a tight fist and I narrowed my gaze.

"Did he say where in Sugarloaf Landing?"

Sugarloaf Landing is a housing community on Lower Sugarloaf Key. I'd never been to it but had driven by many times.

"He said he was at number sixty-two. What's going on here, Logan? Who was that on the phone? Does this have anything to do with—"

"Yes. It has everything to do with that."

He swallowed, then nodded.

"Did this asshole say a time?"

Gus shook his head.

"No set time. Though he did say that if you didn't show by sunset, he'd kill her."

I nodded. I hadn't dealt with a lot of hostage situations in my life, but I'd been trained in the basics. Negotiating with this guy was out of the question, I knew that much. I also knew that the longer that Martha was with him, the greater the chances were that she'd end up dead.

I turned on my heels just as Ange walked over and practically bumped right into her.

"Whoa there, you been sneaking beers without—" She cut herself off when she saw the expression on my face. Hers shifted from playful to serious in an instant. "What's going on?"

"It's Buck Harlan," I said.

I strode by her, heading for the Baia.

"What about him?" Ange said, following right behind me.

"Call Jane," I said as I jumped over the side and onto the deck. "Tell her to meet us here. Make sure she brings backup."

"What's going on?"

"I know where he is," I said, turning back to look at her as she stepped over the gunwale. "And it sounds like Martha's still alive."

Ange followed me down into the main cabin. I told her everything Gus had told me, then she stepped into the galley and called up Jane. I went straight for the small starboard closet to grab my gear for the upcoming confrontation. Back when I was in the Navy, Scott used to call it saddling up. I grabbed my bulletproof vest, strapped it down, and threw a lightweight tee shirt on to conceal it. I had my Sig holstered with a fully loaded mag inserted. It was concealed from view under the right side of my cargo shorts waistband. At the backside of my belt, I strapped down my sheathed spare titanium dive knife. Before stepping out, I grabbed the extra vest so that Ange could wear one as well.

She was just finishing up her call when I stepped out.

"She's on her way," Ange said.

I handed her the vest and she strapped it down. She'd already changed into a pair of cutoff jeans on the boat ride back to town. Her Glock 26 was strapped down in the same place as mine, hidden from view aside from a slight bump.

We locked up the Baia, turned on the security system, then strode down the dock with Atticus right beside us. We headed straight for the office and asked Gus to look after him for a few hours. On our way to the parking lot, we met up with Jack and Pete, who were just finishing up at the cleaning station. They had a pile of fillets wrapped in newspaper and a few buckets of fish guts.

We told them what was going on, and without a thought, they insisted on coming with. We helped them clean up, then headed for the shore. Jane pulled into the lot in a squad car just as we reached the top of the metal ramp. We quickly went over a plan, and once she'd assured me that neither she nor any other officer would go near the house before I did, I gave her the location.

"I'll take the lead," she said. There was a deputy sitting in the passenger seat of her cruiser. She glanced at him, then at the backseat. "Not sure I have enough room for all of you and your gear." She turned her gaze to the mostly empty lot around her and added, "You guys got something that can keep up?"

I looked over at Pete's Camaro, which was parked in the front row, just a few empty spaces down from us. Its shiny polished paint sparkled under the afternoon sun.

"Well, Pete," I said. "You wanted to stretch her legs out. Looks like we've got our chance." I turned back to Jane and added, "We'll be right on your tail."

The three of us headed over to the Camaro. It was even better looking up close. With its sleek garnet-red finish, shiny rims, and new tires, it looked like a show car.

Pete stopped me as I moved toward the passenger side and shook his head. "You drive, boyo. My eyes aren't what they used to be."

He handed me the keys and we all piled in. Pete had completely redone the leather seats and interior paneling. It had a simple yet elegant look. Sliding the key into the ignition, I rotated it forward and listened as the loud and powerful V-8 engine growled to life. The entire car shook as I brought us out of the space and followed Jane out of the lot. She lit up her police lights, blared the siren, and hit the gas.

We followed right behind her as she paved the way, flying out of the lot and down the cross streets toward US-1. When we got out of the city, she floored it ahead of us and we kept right with her, flying over Stock Island at over a hundred miles per

250

hour. The power and speed were incredible, and the ocean and islands flew by in a blur.

As I kept my eyes focused on the road ahead of us, I thought about my enemy. I didn't care how he'd found out who I was and where I kept my boat. I also didn't care why he'd suddenly decided to man up and face me. All I cared about was taking him down before he had a chance to hurt anyone else.

We thundered past the Saddlebunch Keys and pulled off onto Lower Sugarloaf Key. We reached the entrance to the Landing just before 1600, completing a drive that would usually take half an hour in under ten minutes thanks to the police escort. Jane had cut the sirens off a ways back so Buck wouldn't hear them and suspect anything.

We pulled into the visitor lot, parking right beside the office building.

"Looks like your destination's right here," Ange said, pointing at her smartphone.

She had the GPS up, and there was a green pin marking the spot where Buck was supposedly hiding out. It was one of the far southern spots, right on the water of Harris Channel.

I nodded and burned the location into my mind.

"If I'm not back in five minutes, move in," I said.

I opened the door and stepped out.

"Screw that!" Ange snapped. "The second I hear a gunshot or see any kind of trouble, I'm barging in there."

There was no point in arguing with her. She was the only person I'd ever met who was even more stubborn than I was.

"That makes three of us, bro," Jack said from the backseat, motioning to Pete.

"Alright," I said. "Just make sure he doesn't see

anyone else until I've engaged. I don't want to risk him trying to kill Martha."

I stepped out, gave a nod to Jane, then moved down the park's main street, heading south.

The community was big. I estimated that there were a few hundred spaces. A retired couple walked a poodle on the other side of the street. Ahead of me, a group of kids pedaled their bikes in circles while two others shot baskets into a hoop. Everyone was going about a typical August day. They were oblivious to the cold-blooded killer who'd infested their quiet little neighborhood.

As I approached space sixty-two, I did a quick survey of the grounds. The small house was simple and unassuming. A single-wide park model with a back porch that looked out over the channel. Its owners clearly took good care of the house and property. The landscaping was sharp and devoid of weeds, the outside walls of the house looked freshly painted, and the roof appeared to be practically new. I guessed that it belonged to a well-off snowbird couple that spent half of the year up north someplace.

I looked around while walking casually up a cobblestone pathway that led to the front porch. Whatever vehicle Buck had used to get there was nowhere in sight. The small driveway was completely empty and the house didn't have a garage.

I approached the front door cautiously. If Buck Harlan knew my name and where I moored my boat, then it was safe to assume that he knew other things about me as well. He probably knew that I was a SEAL, and even if he didn't, he knew that I could handle myself in a fight. That much was surmisable from our brief encounters back in the Everglades. I wanted to be ready for whatever strategy he had in store. He didn't exactly strike me as the kind of guy who took kindly to a fair fight.

I glanced down at my dive watch. It was 1603, which meant that Gus had gotten off the phone with Buck a little over half an hour ago. I could try and recon the place, sneak around and peek in through the windows. But I decided against it. Buck would be keeping close to Martha. He had the windows open and I knew he'd be watching, listening for any sign of an approaching person. He'd lived years in the swamp, and in that time his ears had undoubtedly grown attuned to notice subtle changes that most people miss. I also didn't want to risk spooking him and putting Martha's life in any more danger than it was already in. So I walked normally and headed straight for the door.

The wooden stairs creaked quietly as I stepped up onto the front porch. A seashell wind chime hung from the rafters and sang in the calm ocean breeze beside me. There was a stuffed animal parrot attached to the door and a woven-rope welcome mat with the words Welcome to Paradise sewn in black letters. I listened carefully, couldn't hear anything inside. Every window's curtains were drawn, even the small one behind the parrot.

I reached for the brass knob with my left hand and turned it. To my surprise, there was no resistance. The mechanism slid smoothly, and the door hinged inward a few inches on its own before I pushed it the rest of the way. I raised my Sig and stepped inside.

My eyes scanned the room for any sign of movement. The shag-carpeted, panel-walled living room appeared empty. The small kitchen as well. It was dark inside. Large drapes blocked light from entering the windows. The only illumination inside the house came from the open door at my back.

I took two steps forward, the soles of my boots transitioning from linoleum to carpet. Then I froze. I heard sounds coming from down the narrow hall across the room. Suddenly, Martha appeared in view. She was practically being dragged from behind by Buck, who had an arm squeezed tight around her upper body. His right hand gripped a large knife, the blade pressed against Martha's neck.

"I told you to come alone, Dodge," Buck yelled.

"I did come alone," I fired right back.

He paused a moment. It had been a bluff on his part. There was no way in hell that he knew about Ange, Jack, Pete, and the police officers at the place's entrance. He'd been trying to get me to screw up. To verify something that he didn't know.

"You stay right fucking there," he snarled as he forced Martha to move. She moaned, so he squeezed her tighter and added, "You stay quiet, bitch."

They stepped out of the shadows and into the dim glow of the living room. Martha looked good, all things considered. She was wearing her tan park ranger pants and a black tank top, both torn up and dirty. Her mouth was gagged with tied-up fabric. Her face was covered in sweat and she shook, scared out of her mind. But aside from a small cut across her forehead, she looked unscathed. Scared, tired, and hungry, but alive.

Buck looked like a madman. His eyes were big and glazed over, looked like he hadn't slept in a week. He'd washed his face, allowing me to see his ugly pit bull–like features without all the dirt and paint. Veins bulged out from his brow and bald head. His jaw was clenched, his nasty yellow teeth on full display. He was wearing the same camo clothes he'd

254

been wearing when we'd met days earlier. I could smell his stench from across the room.

He stopped between a recliner and the kitchen counter. There was only about ten feet separating us. I still had my Sig raised but didn't have a shot. Buck utilized his brute strength to keep Martha's head and body right in front of his.

"Drop the gun or she dies," Buck said.

I didn't have much of a choice. We weren't going to get anywhere if I didn't do as he said. I had to play his game, at least for a little bit.

I kept my eyes forward, staring right at Buck. Lowering my Sig, I bent down and set it on the carpet beside me. I was able to see Buck from a different angle as I leaned down. I saw his holstered silver revolver, the handle barely sticking into view. I also saw what looked like the wooden stock of a sawed-off shotgun on the floor on the other side of the recliner. He'd planned for this, had set the stage so that we'd face off right where we were.

"Kick it away from you," he said angrily.

I nodded slowly and tapped my Sig with my boot, causing it to tumble to the center of the living room.

We stood quiet for a few seconds, staring each other down. He was trying to intimidate me, to strike fear into my bones. It wasn't going to work. Even as a kid, I'd take on the biggest bully on the playground without skipping a beat. I don't get intimidated—just the way I'm hardwired.

"Well?" I said. "I showed up. I kept my end of the bargain. Now it's time to let her go."

He gave an unusual laugh. It wasn't exasperated or sinister in nature. It was just cold and unaffected.

Maybe this guy really is crazy. Maybe he thinks

255

he's somehow in the right here.

"You're not running this, asshole," he growled. "I make the decisions here." He shook his head and added, "You fucked up royally when you killed my brothers."

I could have corrected him. I hadn't actually killed either of them. The first had ended his own life and the second had been eaten by their own pet alligator. I could tell him, but I knew it would only piss him off even more. If it was just the two of us in that house, I probably would have. But it wasn't just the two of us. Martha was there, and I knew that the angrier Buck got, the less likely he'd be to let her walk.

Instead, I said nothing. I let the silence stretch out longer. Let him make the next move.

With my weapon on the floor, he shifted his head around Martha's so that our eyes met. He was thinking hard. His sinister mind was calculating what to do next.

I no longer had my Sig, but my dive knife was sheathed right at my back. I could snatch it and fling it through the air faster than this redneck could blink. A few years ago, I wouldn't have been confident enough to pull it off. But Ange was an expert knife thrower, and she'd worked with me a lot over the past year or so.

Suddenly, his vision narrowed and his breathing quickened.

"You will pay for their deaths," he said. "You will pay for all that you've done, you son of a bitch!"

His voice rose with every word until he was belting out a ferocious yell. He leaned back, slid his arm off Martha, and kicked her hard straight toward me. Her eyes bulged as her weak, terrified body

256

lurched forward.

He was expecting me to catch her, expecting my good Samaritan instincts to take over my reason. I knew his angle. If I caught her, he'd put a succession of .45-caliber rounds right through the both of us. He'd take advantage of my lapse and kill us both. But I didn't catch her.

I shifted away from her and darted toward Buck as he reached for the revolver at his back. He gripped it and managed to raise the barrel halfway to me before I launched my body and tackled him with all of my strength. He grunted as I slammed him back. The breath heaved from his lungs as we both flew through the air, crashing through the thin paneled wall behind him.

We hit the floor hard, his back taking most of the force. We rolled and tumbled against a bed frame, and he hit me across the face with a big meaty fist. My head snapped sideways, but I held tight to his right wrist. He was still clutching his revolver, and he managed to fire off two booming rounds before I twisted my body and snapped his arm over my shoulder.

My ears rang as the weapon fell to the floor. He retaliated by pulling me close and slamming a knee into my chest. I grunted and lurched back, doing my best to absorb the blow.

I threw a punch toward his face, but he weaved sideways in a blur. I was about to knock him on his ass with a slide kick when he dove on top of me. We rolled violently back into the living room, breaking the living room table in our wake and knocking the tackle box to the carpet as we jerked to a stop beside the couch.

He reached for any weapon he could and grabbed

hold of a lamp's power cord. Pulling hard on the cord, he ripped the plug free of its outlet and jolted the lamp from its stand, causing it to shatter beside us.

In a strong, quick motion, he wrapped the cord around my neck and pulled with all his strength. I gasped for air as the cord crunched against my trachea.

My vision grew blurry, and I saw stars spinning around me. He had my body pinned in an awkward position. In a last-ditch effort, I reached around me for any possible weapon I could use against him. Just as I felt my consciousness begin to fade, my left hand rummaged through the open tackle box and grabbed hold of a pair of needle-nose pliers.

Aiming the metal tip toward Buck, I slammed it into his upper chest as hard as I could. The jaws slammed deep into his flesh, causing his body to lurch in pain and his face to wince. As he growled in pain and blood flowed out from the wound, I pulled the cord off my neck, jumped to my feet, and hit him square in his big belly with a powerful front kick. He fell back into the entertainment center, his heavy frame cracking the television and shattering the stand to pieces.

He hit the floor hard and tumbled against the wall. Rolling over onto his back, he ripped the pliers from his chest with a grunt, then snatched a pointy piece of the broken television stand. I glanced down at the recliner, bent over and grabbed the sawed-off shotgun. Before he'd recovered to his feet, I had the two barrels staring at him. He froze in front of the living room window, wiping the blood from his mouth.

I didn't say anything. Didn't have to. My eyes met his, my expression saying more than words ever could. My rage was fuming. I saw something primal and ancient when he looked back at me. He had a primitive look of fear in his eyes, like that of a cornered wild animal. It lasted only a fraction of a second. That was all it took for me to squeeze the trigger, and for the mechanical operation to take place. The spring action of the hammer, the strike to the primer, the ignition of the gunpowder. A loud, powerful boom that shook the whole house.

A wave of lead pellets struck the center of his flabby body in an instant. Blood sprayed out from his chest, and the force knocked him off his feet, hurling him backward into the window. The glass shattered as his big frame tore out into the hot air. He flipped around, performing a full 360 before slamming hard into the flower pots and gravel driveway below.

I stepped over to the shattered window and cocked the shotgun. I was ready to fire off another shell, just in case the first one hadn't completely wiped the life from him. I didn't want there to be any chance of him being swept off to the nearest hospital for urgent care. I wanted the whole thing to end, right then and there.

I didn't need to fire another shell. His body was mangled. His midsection was blown to shreds. Organs rested outside his shredded, bloodied skin. He wasn't moving. He wasn't breathing. The deed had been done, and done without question.

I set the shotgun on the floor and turned around. Martha was crouched against the far wall. She was shaking in fear, crying like mad, and breathing heavily. She was still blindfolded and gagged.

I caught my breath, then strode over to her.

"It's okay, Martha," I said, speaking clearly so that she knew that it was me who'd won the fight.

I dropped down beside her and placed a hand softly on her shoulder. She jerked back instinctively.

"It's me, Logan Dodge," I said. I took a deep breath and added, "You don't have to worry about him anymore, Martha. He's gone."

She relaxed a little, and I removed her blindfold and gag. Her eyes were wide and watery. She scanned around the room, then looked over at me.

"Is he... dead?" she said through labored breaths.

Her pulse was like a jackhammer. Probably well over a hundred beats per minute.

"Yes," I said softly. "You're safe now, Martha."

THIRTY-TWO

Ange was the first one through the door. She stormed in with her Glock raised and her head on a swivel like a member of a SWAT team. She was focused and unafraid of putting her life on the line. A real warrior woman.

She relaxed a little when she made eye contact with me.

"Where's Buck?" she said, her mind and body in attack mode.

I nodded toward the shattered window across from me. "I put him down."

She strode across the living room and looked out through the window frame. Her eyes took in the scene for a few seconds before she turned around and headed over to me.

"Are you alright?" she said, holstering her Glock and kneeling down beside me.

"My ears will be ringing for a few days," I said. "And I'm sure Buck added a few scars to my collection, but I'm fine."

She placed one hand over my shoulder and the other around Martha.

"Martha, are you okay?" she said.

Martha nodded, her body still shaking. She'd been through a lot, and I knew that it would take a long time for her to get over it. If she ever did.

Ange kissed my forehead and tightened her grasp on me.

Jack entered next, followed right behind by Pete, Jane, and a handful of other officers.

The place quickly turned into a madhouse, with officers, detectives, and EMTs all over the place. There was a lot of work to do. A guy was lying dead and mutilated in a well-populated housing complex. They quickly taped off the crime scene to keep locals away. People all over the island had heard the three gunshots. A large group of them had gathered around to see what all the fuss was about. Their peaceful slice of island paradise had been disturbed, and they wanted to know the whos and whys.

Fortunately, we had an excuse to get out of there promptly. Though I wasn't seriously injured, Jane and Ange insisted I go to the hospital. I was faced with either sitting there and answering question after question or lying up in a hospital bed. I chose the lesser of the two evils, and Ange drove me down to the Lower Keys Medical Center with Jack and Pete in the backseat. I knew that I was only delaying the inevitable, that the hours and hours of questioning would come and find me no matter what.

After a few hours at the hospital, my primary physician, Dr. Patel, gave me the all clear. He said I'd be fine, that the ringing would go away in a day or two and that I was lucky I hadn't ruptured an eardrum. He seemed more concerned with the dog wounds I'd sustained the previous day to my chest and shoulder. A few of the cuts across my chest had opened up, so he sanitized the wounds and restitched them.

Once done at the hospital, we headed over to the police station to meet with Jane and a few detectives. I told them all about how Buck Harlan had given me a message to meet him at that house alone. It was a long couple of hours of questions, but Jane did her best to get me out of there. A serial killer had been killed and no one had been injured. It was a win all the way around, as good of an outcome as could've been expected.

That evening we cruised downtown to Sloppy Joes to meet up with Jack, Pete, Cal, and a few other local friends. We ate piles of delicious seafood while washing it all down with beer and cocktails. Even Billy managed to make it down to our island paradise for the evening and our group told stories and celebrated while enjoying some of the best food around.

I stepped out for a few minutes when I got a phone call from Scott, who expressed his disappointment that I'd taken down the bad guys before he'd been able to get away from his responsibilities and fly down there.

"Maybe next time I'll make it down there," he said. "Can't let you have all the fun, chief."

I laughed. "Next time? Don't think I'll be taking on any more serial killers anytime soon."

"Doesn't have to be serial killers," he replied. "Could be drug kingpins, gangsters, corrupt businessmen. It's just a matter of time with you, Logan."

We talked for a few more minutes, then I

rejoined the group and filled my stomach even more. After dinner, I felt tired and decided to call it an early night.

Ange and I sat out in our backyard and relaxed while watching the sunset. We lay on the hammock together, watching the vibrant colors shift across the sky while I tired out Atticus with a tennis ball.

As the sunset sky was at its zenith, Ange turned to me and smiled. I had my arm around her and she had a bare leg draped over me.

"It was a good thing you did today, Logan," she said. "Helping Martha and going after that killer."

"You would've done the exact same thing if you'd been in my place," I told her.

She nodded. "Yeah. But I wasn't in your place. You were the one who stepped up, who put yourself in danger to face that guy one on one." She locked her blue eyes on to mine. "I know none of this will bring back the Shepherds, but I also know that they'd both be damn proud of what you've done. And South Florida can feel safer now knowing that those guys are gone. Who knows how many others would be dead in the future if it wasn't for you?"

"If it wasn't for us, you mean," I said. "You're forgetting that you're the one who took out that brother on their island. None of this would have happened without you, Ange."

She smiled and laid her head on my chest.

"How is it possible that I fall more in love with you every day?" she said.

I kissed her forehead. "I was about to ask the same question."

We fell asleep right there on the hammock as the sky shifted to darkness. Ange was intoxicating. Her smell, the sound of her voice, the feel of her skin

264

against mine. I'd made a lot of mistakes in my life, but she was living proof that I was capable of making good decisions at least every now and then. Marrying her was the best thing I'd ever done.

Over the next couple of weeks, things gradually returned to normal. We'd been away on our honeymoon for three months and had been swept up into a deadly conflict the day we'd gotten back. Now we were settling in, getting back into our normal island life routine. Our days were filled with trips out exploring the islands, scuba diving, and freediving for lobster. As my injuries healed, I worked my way back into my daily workout routine. Running, swimming, high-speed interval training, and sessions on the heavy bag.

In mid-September, we motored up to Tavernier for the Lionfish Derby and Festival. A few locals had conjured the idea of the friendly competition in order to help rid the islands of the invasive species that was having a strong negative effect on the marine ecosystem. There are few activities that can top spearfishing and helping the environment at the same time. And the colorful fish tastes good too, so long as you can fillet it without getting poked by its venomous, razor-sharp spines.

On the boat ride back to Key West, I throttled the Baia up to her cruising speed of forty knots. Jack was playing with Atticus on the sunbed behind me. Ange was sprawled out on the bow, her lean, tanned body looking like it belonged on the cover of the *Sports Illustrated* Swimsuit Edition.

I leaned back into the cushioned seat, held on to the wheel with one hand and eased the throttles forward with the other. I took a bite of the savory grilled lionfish, then washed it down with a few swigs of chilled Paradise Sunset beer. The water glistened around us in the late-afternoon sun, and the warm breeze rushed through my hair. I smiled and nodded. All was well in paradise once more.

THE END

Logan Dodge Adventures

Gold in the Keys
(Florida Keys Adventure Series Book 1)

Hunted in the Keys
(Florida Keys Adventure Series Book 2)

Revenge in the Keys
(Florida Keys Adventure Series Book 3)

Betrayed in the Keys
(Florida Keys Adventure Series Book 4)

Redemption in the Keys
(Florida Keys Adventure Series Book 5)

Corruption in the Keys
(Florida Keys Adventure Series Book 6)

Predator in the Keys
(Florida Keys Adventure Series Book 7)

If you're interested in receiving my newsletter for updates on my upcoming books, you can sign up on my website:

matthewrief.com

About the Author

Matthew has a deep-rooted love for adventure and the ocean. He loves traveling, diving, rock climbing and writing adventure novels. Though he grew up in the Pacific Northwest, he currently lives in Virginia Beach with his wife, Jenny.

Made in the USA
Monee, IL
22 May 2025